THE ULTIMATE BOOK OF
MOVIE MONSTERS

I want to dedicate this book to my family and friends. Thank you all for your excitement and support. It means the world to me.

For my mother, Patricia, and my father Dave, for being massive horror fans and passing on your love of all things terrifying and spooky to me and my brothers. I promise we're (mostly) well adjusted. I love you so much.

For my brothers, Graham and David, for watching all of these disgusting, hilarious and terrifying movies with me throughout the years, and always warning me when the scariest parts were coming. You two are "Groovy", and I love you both.

For Dawn, my partner in crime, fellow horror lover and my best friend in the whole world. Your love and encouragement helped motivate me to keep writing and pursuing my dreams. You are the kindest, most loving wife and mother in the world, and anyone who crosses your path is all the better for it. I'm the luckiest man alive to get to spend my days with you. I love you so much.

For Aurora, Bram and Fia, my own little monsters. You light up my days. You are funny, intelligent, kind and loving, and every day with you is pure joy. I love you all more than anything in the world, and you make me proud every single day. I hope this book doesn't traumatise you!

THE ULTIMATE BOOK OF
MOVIE
MONSTERS

CHRISTOPHER CARTON

WHITE OWL

AN IMPRINT OF PEN & SWORD BOOKS LTD.
YORKSHIRE – PHILADELPHIA

First published in Great Britain in 2022 by
Pen and Sword WHITE OWL
An imprint of
Pen & Sword Books Ltd
Yorkshire - Philadelphia

ISBN 978 1 39909 682 9

A CIP catalogue record for this book is available from the British Library.

Movie images credited to Movie Stills Database

Typeset in 12/16 pts Cormorant Infant
by SJmagic DESIGN SERVICES, India.

Printed and bound in India by Replika Press Pvt. Ltd.

Pen & Sword Books Ltd incorporates the imprints of Pen & Sword Books Archaeology,
Atlas, Aviation, Battleground, Discovery, Family History, History, Maritime, Military,
Naval, Politics, Railways, Select, Transport, True Crime, Fiction, Frontline Books, Leo
Cooper, Praetorian Press, Seaforth Publishing, Wharncliffe and White Owl.

For a complete list of Pen & Sword titles please contact

PEN & SWORD BOOKS LIMITED
47 Church Street, Barnsley, South Yorkshire, S70 2AS, England
E-mail: enquiries@pen-and-sword.co.uk
Website: www.pen-and-sword.co.uk

or

PEN AND SWORD BOOKS
1950 Lawrence Rd, Havertown, PA 19083, USA
E-mail: Uspen-and-sword@casematepublishers.com
Website: www.penandswordbooks.com

CONTENTS

INTRODUCTION

Fear has been an integral part of cinema for over a century. Filmmakers have sought to thrill us in a myriad of ways in that time. They create stories which deal with real-world problems and force us to face our mortality. They bring us action-packed and adrenaline-fueled spectacle and place our favourite characters in jeopardy for our entertainment. They tackle societal issues and traumatic events of the past with respect and harrowing realism. But one of the most common and effective ways in which directors and writers tap into our psyches and raise hairs on the back of our necks, is by placing us face to face with monsters.

Some of the most recognisable forces in the industry have been the creatures conjured up from the darkest and most imaginative places in the minds of filmmakers. From towering behemoths to shuffling corpses to otherworldly abominations, the monsters of cinema have burrowed their way into the hearts and souls of movie-goers around the world.

Destructive, terrifying, deadly and craving for bloodshed and mayhem, these beasts have wreaked havoc globally and always seem to come back for more. But some are protectors, using their power or magic to defend us, to oppose the beasts that try to scare us. And some are misunderstood; only monsters in the eyes of those who don't comprehend them. Some are simply mischievous, prancing ghouls who serve to make these stories eerie and abnormal.

There are thousands of monsters in all sizes and forms that have shaped the landscape of film across every genre, from disaster movies to fantasy adventures, gory body-horror pictures and heartfelt family dramas. The following are some of the most iconic, unique, inventive and terrifying creatures to ever grace a screen. Monster is a relative term, but that being said, some of the creatures to come might have you sleeping with your head under the covers and all the lights on.

CHAPTER 1

VICIOUS VAMPIRES

A shadow looms above you as you follow the same shortcut you've used every single day. Your footsteps echo through the alleyway as you quicken your pace, certain your mind is playing tricks. A flutter of wings. Birds looking for scraps... You pull your collar tight and speed up again, praying no one sees you looking anxious and silly. The hairs on your neck stand up. A presence... You can feel the eyes piercing the back of your skull, yet now you are frozen. Locked in place by a paralysing fear that has chilled your bones and makes you feel as though your blood runs cold. But it's not cold... it's pumping warm tonight, and it's flowing from your neck and into the dead, waiting lips of the cursed... the living undead. Your pulse slows with each drop the pearly fangs drain from

Vampire by Edvard Munch

your supple neck, and slowly you drift into the ether. Will your life cease? Will you awaken to find you have become one with the cursed, destined to live a tormented life of unending thirst? And if those are your choices, which would be worse?

Vampire

Common Strengths	: Shape-shifting, sharp fangs to satiate the thirst for blood, psychological manipulation, immortality.
Common Weaknesses	: Sunlight, garlic, holy water, piercing of the heart, decapitation.

With their history steeped in the gothic literature of the nineteenth century, the dreaded vampire treads a fine line between paralysing fear and morbid intrigue. Since the publication of John William Polidori's *The Vampyre* in 1819, vampires have sunk their teeth into horror-fiction in a massive way, becoming staple monsters in the genre. By virtue of this, the fanged fiends would inevitably make their presence known on a cinematic scale.

THE COUNT...

Dracula

Created by	: Bram Stoker
Appearances	: Countless incarnations of the Dracula story, Hollywood mash-ups such as *Van Helsing* and *Monster Squad*.

Bram Stoker's horror masterpiece, *Dracula*, truly brought the characteristics of the modern vampire into the mainstream. The callous Count was a cold and unfeeling character, treating main protagonist Jonathan Harker with an eerie and mostly unspoken passive-aggressive slight, feigning interest while also holding the solicitor to ransom with his clever word play and dominant demeanour.

The physical traits we all now see as synonymous with blood-sucking beasts were prevalent in the novel, such as his deathly weakness to sunlight, his insatiable thirst for human blood and his ability to shape-shift at will. Likewise, Count Dracula utilised his cunning and charm, as well as his resident seductive concubines, to bend his victims to his will and influence their very souls. Because of the uneasy and palpable terror in Stoker's novel, the appeal of his story wasn't long being adapted for film.

The very first movie to feature this iconic monster was the 1921 horror film *Dracula's Death*. While it may have taken some influence from the novel, it was actually a wholly original story. However, the movie is now generally regarded as a lost film, although writer Troy Howarth mentions in his book, *Tome of Terror* (2016), that a print of the film still exists in a Hungarian archive.

In 1922, the now-iconic masterpiece *Nosferatu* was released. This silent film featured elements that were almost identical to the story of *Dracula*, albeit with names replaced and certain events reshuffled, presumably in order to avoid legal wrangles (nevertheless, Stoker's estate still brought legal action against the filmmakers). In the movie, Count Orlock shares some similarities with Stoker's character, such as sleeping in a coffin, craving the blood of the living and avoiding the sunlight.

This haunting film is bathed in an unsettling atmosphere, one which is exacerbated by the fact that it is silent. All that accompanies the dancing shadows and lurking figures is an eclectic score that tinkles along with the horror on screen. While it might not terrify in quite the same way today, Max Schreck gave a chilling performance as the Count. His gangly form seems to leap from the screen, and the scene in which Orlock ascends the staircase, seen only as a shadow, is masterful in its suspense. Thomas Hutter has every right to huddle in his quarters and hope that the dreaded vampire Lord doesn't enter the bedroom...

Even though it may not have the official blessing of the Stoker estate, *Nosferatu* still has its place as one of the most influential monster movies of all time.

Dracula would make one of his most famous appearances in a film adaptation of the theatre version of Stoker's novel. Iconic horror actor Bela Lugosi took on the role in a much more faithful version of the Dracula story. Wooden stakes, hypnotism and shape-shifting all make an appearance in this

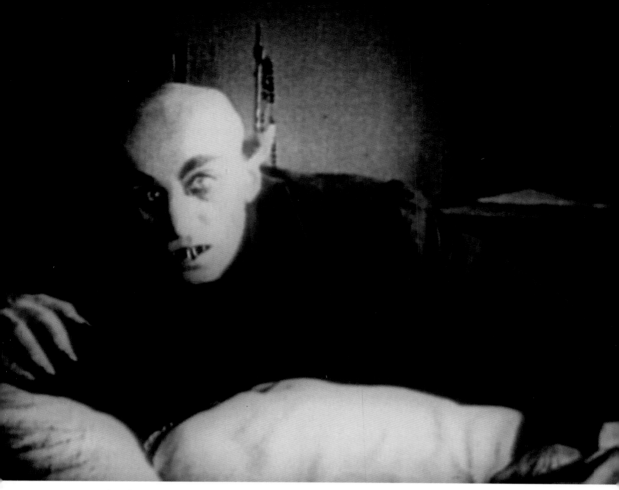

Max Schreck as Count Orlock – © Film Arts Guild

stripped back, atmospheric relic of the golden age of black and white horror. Bela Lugosi has rightfully earned his reputation as a dealer of suspense, as his Dracula is a hypnotic and intimidating vampire Lord who commands his tongue and his teeth with equal power.

While many sequels to this seminal film were released, only one other movie had Lugosi in the role of Count Dracula. *Abbott and Costello Meet Frankenstein* (1948) saw the bumbling duo cross paths with Dracula, as well as Frankenstein's monster and the Wolf Man.

The fearsome Count made another, notably more terrifying appearance in a 1958 version of *Dracula*, from legendary horror studio, Hammer. The traits of the vicious vampire remained much the same, save for the usual transformations into bat or wolf form, but with the advancement of film technology it allowed for a more tense and atmospheric experience. Christopher Lee took on the

THE ULTIMATE BOOK OF MOVIE MONSTERS

Bela Lugosi as Dracula – © Universal Pictures

role of the demonic vampire in this, and six further movies that followed, and he was praised for his intimidating screen presence. This version of *Dracula* featured more seductive undertones, playing on the idea of the blood-sucking demons and their nocturnal habits as being of an innately sexual nature.

Francis Ford Coppola brought a more visceral and modern take on the *Dracula* mythos to film in 1991 with *Bram Stoker's Dracula*. The big-budget horror

Christopher Lee as Dracula – © Universal Pictures

Gary Oldman as Vlad the Impaler/Dracula – © Colombia Pictures

THE ULTIMATE BOOK OF MOVIE MONSTERS

film starred Gary Oldman in an iconic take on the Count, as well as Keanu Reeves as Jonathan Harker and Winona Ryder as Mina. Oldman's Dracula was given a substantial backstory, once being the war hungry Vlad the Impaler, which made the creepy goings-on at the castle much more effective.

This gothic picture was notably faithful to the source material for the most part, and the modern special effects made for some terrifying imagery, particularly when the Count crawls about the walls of his castle, when he transforms into a wolf and, subsequently, a human-sized bat which bursts into a multitude of rats. With mostly practical effects used on screen, Coppola's movie is successful in keeping the horror more in line with the classics of cinema, rather than adopting the plethora of new, digital technologies that were becoming abundant in the film industry at the time.

Dracula in wolf form – © Colombia Pictures

Dracula's multiple guises throughout the movie truly show the effectiveness of this most domineering of creatures. Whether he is leading the charge on the fields of battle, trying to sneak a taste of blood from his unsuspecting 'guests', or taking flight as a winged creature of the night, this version of Dracula is fully rounded and utterly unsettling.

Dracula returned in various forms throughout the decade, and while he was known mostly for his villainous nature, some of his other appearances took on more heroic and even comedic slants. In Mel Brooks' spoof film *Dracula: Dead and Loving It* (1995), Leslie Nielsen played the Count in a slapstick caper that spoofed both the novel and the various film iterations of the vampire Lord. Similarly, the *Hotel Transylvania* series of animated movies showcases 'Drac's' insecurities as a father and the owner of the eponymous hotel. Adam Sandler puts on his best Transylvanian accent to portray the not-so-vicious vampire as he struggles with a human entering his daughter Mavis' life.

In 2014, Dracula was given a slightly more heroic role in the film *Dracula Untold*. Rather than re-treading the novel or the storylines explored in previous adaptations, this movie saw Vlad Dracula (Luke Evans) choosing to bring a curse upon himself in order to protect those he cares about. Seeing Dracula using his powers in a war-torn setting offers different insight into this monster, giving him a humanity that has been touched upon briefly before, but never

Dracula – © Colombia Pictures

Mavis Dracula (Selena Gomez) and Count Dracula (Adam Sandler) in Hotel Transylvania – © Sony Pictures Releasing

given this amount of depth and reasoning. The action-packed dark adventure shows the control and sacrifices asked of the Impaler, and makes some of his more fantastical powers even more effective.

Now living in the public zeitgeist arguably more than any other movie monster, the dreaded Count Dracula continues to strike fear and draw intrigue from the hearts of film-goers and monster enthusiasts. Over the last century, he has earned his place as the definitive vampire. But he certainly isn't the only one...

Luke Evans as Vlad in Dracula Untold – © Universal Pictures

BLOODTHIRST AND LUST...

Fran and Miriam

Created by : Diana Daubeney
Appearances : *Vampyres* (1974)

As the decades moved on, among the multiple sequels to feature Dracula, sub-genres of a more overtly sexual nature emerged. The novella *Carmella* (1872), one of the early examples of vampiric literature, contained subtle homosexual undertones, being one of the first examples of the lesbian vampire trope. It was adapted for film as *Blood and Roses* in 1960 by director Roger Vadim. A movie such as *Vampyres* (1974) featured more violence and graphic sexual content than previous vampire films. It followed two female vampire antagonists who were romantically involved with each other as they preyed on their victims in their run-down home.

While the forbidden sexual nature of the vampire continued to play a role in the decades to come, the '80s brought with it a more campy and stylish

Miriam (Anulka Dziubinska) and Fran (Marianne Morris) in Vampyres – © Cambist Films

Amy Peterson (Amanda Bearse) in Fright Night – © *Colombia Pictures*

form of vampire in cult films such as *Fright Night* (1985) and *The Lost Boys* (1987). In *Fright Night*, Charley Brewster, a horror fan, discovers that his next-door neighbour is a vampire. He tries to enlist a movie-star-turned-TV host to aid him in ending the cruel vampire's killing spree.

Jerry Dandridge

Created by : Tom Holland
Appearances : *Fright Night* (1985), *Fright Night* (2011)

Fright Night's villain, Jerry, has many of the stereotypical traits of the cinematic vampire. He is manipulative and disparaging, he has a weakness to sunlight, he shows no reflection when faced with a mirror, and he cannot enter a premises without express invitation from the owner. The movie has gained popularity over the years for its unique blend of comedy and horror, and spawned a sequel,

Jerry Dandridge (Chris Sarandon) in Fright Night – © Colombia Pictures

a remake and a sequel to the remake. A direct follow-up to the original movie, tentatively titled *Fright Night: Resurrection*, is due to be released in the future.

David & Marko

Created by : Janice Fischer and James Jeremias

Appearances : *The Lost Boys* (1987), *Lost Boys: Reign of Frogs* (2008 – *David*, comic book mini-series)

The cult classic *The Lost Boys* (1987), a staple of '80s comedy-horror, brought with it a new and now-iconic crew of fanged fiends. The film follows brothers Michael and Sam Emerson, who, upon moving to Santa Carla in California, cross paths with a biker gang who are actually a group of vampires who have begun preying on the town's residents. This stylish movie blends genres well, keeping a lighter, campy tone when the story calls for it, but still ensuring

Kiefer Sutherland in The Lost Boys – © Warner Bros. Pictures

the vampiric threat is a real and engaging one. Kiefer Sutherland plays
one of the most prominent vampires, David, who continues the cinematic
trend of being a manipulative and powerful being whose devious nature
has deadly consequences for the living. David and his gang are merciless in
their quest for blood, and the movie deftly balances light-hearted jokes with
genuine horror.

David and his crew carry many of the now stereotypical traits of vampires
such as an aversion to holy water and garlic, and an immediate fatality
when pierced through the heart. The movie does bring an interesting concept
into the proceedings when Sam must work with the Frog brothers (Santa

Alex Winter in The Lost Boys *– © Warner Bros. Pictures*

Carla's resident vampire hunters) to find and defeat the 'head vampire' and, in doing so, rescue Sam's brother Michael from his half-vampiric state, whereby he has not fully transformed but is sensitive to light and has a nagging craving for human blood. Michael treads the line of monstrosity, as he retains his human morals and strength of character, but battles with the newfound power and temptations of his impending transformation. *The Lost Boys* is a great film for showcasing the very well-preserved human nature of these monsters. While otherworldly creatures and merciless abominations with only a will to kill are terrifying in and of themselves, the variety in styles of vampires which have become prominent on film and in literature for the better part of a century generally melds a terrifying psychological power with violent, super-human advantages.

LESTAT DE LIONCOURT...

Lestat de Lioncourt

Created by : Anne Rice

Appearances : *Interview with the Vampire* (1994), *Queen of the Damned* (2002)

The late Anne Rice adapted her own novel, *Interview with the Vampire*, for film in 1994. Starring Tom Cruise as Lestat – a recurring main character in her extremely popular *Vampire Chronicles* novel series – the movie had a nuanced and character-driven approach to vampirism. The film is framed around an interview with Louis, a vampire played by Brad Pitt, as he chronicles his life events, specifically his dealings with the vampire Lestat, the one responsible for biting and turning Louis in 1791.

While the film has its share of violence owing to Lestat's penchant for hunting and killing humans, treating it as a type of sport, it also spends a satisfying amount of time building the relationship Louis and Lestat share as a reluctant student and twisted mentor. This relationship is made all the more complicated with the turning and subsequent informal adoption of Claudia (Kirsten Dunst), a small girl that Louis feeds from in desperation, and Lestat then turns to keep her in their company eternally.

Tom Cruise as Lestat in Interview with the Vampire *– © Warner Bros. Pictures*

Unique for its deep-dive into the regrets that are abundant in the immortal life of a vampire, the movie mixes heartbreak, period-drama, violence and intrigue to make a picture that has a well-earned place in the annals of monster movie history. Stuart Townsend would go on to play the role of Lestat in *Queen of the Damned* (2002), another *Vampire Chronicles* film, which saw Lestat's interactions with an ancient vampire called Akasha, played by the late 'Princess of R'n'B', Aaliyah.

LET'S GET TO RAMBLING...

Vampires

Created by : Robert Rodriguez and Quentin Tarantino
Appearances : *From Dusk Till Dawn* (1996), From *Dusk Till Dawn 2: Texas Blood Money* (1999), *From Dusk Till Dawn 3: The Hangman's Daughter* (2000), *From Dusk Till Dawn: The Series* (2014–2016. TV series on El Rey Network and Netflix)

In 1996, Robert Rodriguez directed a prominent vampire movie called *From Dusk Till Dawn*, which brought with it some of the most aggressive vampires in cinema. When criminal brothers Seth and Richie Gecko take a family hostage in order to cross the Mexican–American border, the group ends up taking a pit-stop at a boisterous bar where things soon take a fatal turn. This classic film is notable for meshing genres seamlessly, so much so that if anyone watched it without knowing any prior information, they would be absolutely shocked at the events that transpire in the doomed road-side bar. The movie again blends horror with tongue-in-cheek humour, thanks to the script by Quentin Tarantino (who also co-stars as Richie Gecko, the mentally disturbed brother of George Clooney's Seth Gecko).

On show are typical newly-turned vampires who still retain much of their human physique and appearance, and fully transformed, unholy beasts who seek to drain every last drop of blood from any unlucky patrons. The typical

Vampires in From Dusk Till Dawn *– © Dimension Films*

weaknesses of vampires are found in *From Dusk Till Dawn*, but thanks to a fantastic script and a genuine sense of fear and hopelessness, the movie succeeds beyond cliché and has become a cult classic.

THE RELUCTANT HERO...

Blade

Created by : Marv Wolfman and Gene Colan

Appearances : *Blade* (1998), *Blade II* (2002), *Blade: Trinity* (2004), *Blade: The Series* (2006), *Blade* (New Marvel Cinematic Universe film, starring Mahershala Ali)

In 1998, the *Blade* film trilogy started with the original installment starring Wesley Snipes as the eponymous vampire hunter. One of Marvel Comics' most intriguing heroes, Blade is a human-vampire hybrid, his mother having been bitten by a vampire before giving birth to him. Blade has been cursed with the urge to drink blood, but otherwise remains human, giving him a distinct advantage when facing fully-vampiric foes. The trilogy concerns Blade's ongoing quest to hunt vampires who seek dominance over humanity, as well as his struggles in continuing to repress his ever-growing monstrous urges. Throughout the trilogy he is aided by various cohorts, but his main ally is Abraham Whistler, played by Kris Kristofferson.

Blade is portrayed by Snipes as cold and efficient, holding a deep resentment for what happened to his mother and in turn cursed him to a life of inhumanity. Whistler aids him by creating new and inventive weapons to dispose of the vampire foes with more ease, preying on their inherent weaknesses. He is similar to other monstrous movie anti-heroes of the time, preceded by the leader of Hell's Army in *Spawn* in 1997 and also by the DC Comics monster hero, *Swamp Thing* in 1982. Joining the ranks of heroic comic-book monsters after Blade was the wise-cracking paranormal agent, *Hellboy* (2004). Utilising the powers of the vampire in a dual role shared between the hero and the main villains helped *Blade* to stand out and remain a unique and action-packed series.

Wesley Snipes as Blade – © New Line Cinema

WHITEOUT...

Vampires (*30 Days of Night*)

Created by : Steve Niles

Appearances : *30 Days of Night* (2007), *30 Days of Night: Blood Trails* (2007 – Mini-series), *30 Days of Night: Dust to Dust* (2008 – Mini-series), *30 Days of Night: Dark Days* (2010)

The seemingly eternal dark of *30 Days of Night* (2007) is the perfect breeding ground for the creatures of the night. Set in Barrow, a small town in Alaska, as the month-long night sets in, the movie sees Josh Hartnett as Sheriff Eben Oleson, who must overcome insurmountable odds as the town is overrun by deadly vampires. Utilising the cloak of darkness, the fanged fiends are free to roam about the snow-covered buildings and pick off unsuspecting townsfolk.

Arvin (Andrew Stehlin) in 30 Days of Night – © Sony Pictures Releasing

The creatures of the night that terrorise the town of Barrow are unrelenting, with black eyes and large, dagger-like fangs. With no daylight, the movie is beyond bleak as the survivors attempt to wait out the darkness and the demons dwelling within it. The blood leeches aren't the only threat to deal with, as tension within the group threatens to give away their location and leave them susceptible to a grim fate.

FORBIDDEN LOVE...

Eli & Abby

Created by   : John Ajvide Lindqvist
Appearances : *Let the Right One In* (2008 – Eli), *Let Me In* (2010 – Abby)

The forbidden love of the vampire was explored in John Ajvide Lindqvist's novel *Let the Right One In* (2004). A tale of both terror and innocence, it deals

Lina Leandersson in Let the Right One In *– © Sandrew Metronome*

with the developing relationship between Oskar, a meek 12-year-old boy, and Eli, a young girl by appearance, who is actually a centuries-old vampire. The novel was adapted into the 2008 feature film of the same name, which Lindqvist also wrote the screenplay for. The Swedish film was haunting and minimalistic, the cold and atmospheric Blackeberg in Stockholm being the perfect setting for the tragic tale of love and fear.

It was also adapted into the American movie *Let Me In*, which keeps a lot of the novel and Swedish film's themes and story beats intact, but alters the setting to New Mexico, and changes the main characters to Owen and Abby. These stories give the main 'monster' perhaps the most humane treatment possible as regards the emotional draw for readers and audience members. Eli and Abby are hauntingly gentle with their words, a front that betrays their inherent, darkest needs. Unlike any previous vampires seen on film, the connections made between the young girl and boy feel real – a genuine spark that seems to have no insidious nature behind it. As such, the storytelling versatility of these creatures is truly unleashed in a way that transcends simply attacking an unwilling victim to satiate a primal need. By the time any true horror is unleashed in both *Let the Right One In* and *Let Me In*, enough emotional groundwork has been laid to ensure audience members feel the tragedy deep in their hearts.

Chloë Grace Moretz in Let Me In *– © Relativity Media*

AND SO THE LION FELL IN LOVE WITH THE LAMB...

Edward Cullen

Created by : Stephanie Meyer

Appearances : *Twilight* (2008), *The Twilight Saga: New Moon* (2009), *The Twilight Saga: Eclipse* (2010), *The Twilight Saga: Breaking Dawn – Part 1* (2011), *The Twilight Saga: Breaking Dawn – Part 2* (2012)

Vampirism played a key role in the thrilling love story between Bella Swan and Edward Cullen in Stephanie Meyer's massively successful novel *Twilight*, and its three sequels. The movie adaptations honoured this relationship, mostly doing away with the simmering evil of the living undead, and instead focusing on

Bella Swan (Kristen Stewart) and Edward Cullen (Robert Pattinson) in Twilight *– © Summit Entertainment*

forbidden desires felt by the two leads. As Edward, one of the Cullen family of vampires, only consumes animal blood, his interest in Bella mostly remains purely romantic. He spends the movie saga defending her, both her honour and her physical safety, as their lives are continually threatened by dangerous and manipulative vampires that kill for sport, as well as vying for her love against a werewolf called Jacob (Taylor Lautner).

The vampires in *The Twilight Saga* buck the majority of stereotypical traits associated with most versions of these classic monsters. Throughout the series, they show various powers, such as super strength and speed, telepathy and a keen sense of premonition. In contrast to the norm, they can live freely in the sunlight, and their skin sparkles like diamonds due to their tough, marble-like exterior. Vampires in this series are presented as hunters, given an alluring scent and perfect features with which to draw in prey.

WOULD IT CHANGE ANYTHING?...

The Girl

Created by : Ana Lily Amirpour
Appearances : *A Girl Walks Home Alone at Night* (2014)

The slow-burn Iranian vampire movie, *A Girl Walks Home Alone at Night* (2014) is unlike any vampire movie that went before. The lonesome, skateboarding 'girl' traverses the Iranian ghost town of 'Bad City', searching for the most morally depraved people to feed off. Like *Blade*, she is somewhat of an anti-hero, once again casting off the shackles of the typical 'monster' that feeds from a primal instinct. Instead, the girl keeps a keen eye on the goings-on in the city, from drug-dealing to blatant misogyny, and deals with culprits who cross her wavering set of morals.

Moody and skewed towards style, the film uses the girl's vampirism sparingly, preferring to keep audience members on edge as characters interact more with

A Girl Walks Home Alone at Night – © *Vice Films*

what they don't say than with the dialogue they're given. Atmosphere is key, and the cinematography that frames the girl's adventures gives the movie a dream-like quality, a subtle attitude that is juxtaposed with what is effectively a lesson in subdued, stylish filmmaking.

That's not to say there aren't monstrous qualities to the movie – she is a vampire after all – but the focus on this melancholia is in the film's favour when it comes to standing on its own within the vampire sub-genre of horror. Its too-cool-for-school attitude might feel a little on the nose or forced for some, but in an already over-bloated genre, what's wrong with having something a little bit different?

Vampires are classic monsters of cinema. They keep most of their humanity, but couple those traits with seriously uncontrollable and often fatal desires. The monsters listed above are but the tip of the iceberg across all mediums for these blood-sucking devils. Other movies such as John Carpenter's western-influenced *Vampires* (1998) and the long-running *Underworld* series offer classic, action-packed takes on the ever-popular monsters. The latter spans multiple movies, and deals with an eternal war between vampires and werewolves, known as lycans. Kate Beckinsale's vampiric Selene is the emotional anchor for the series, and though she is a vampire, she reflects emotion and heroism like few others in the genre. Overall, vampires remain enthralling for their ability to show so much humanity, while remaining monstrous beneath the veil. Sometimes, the most terrifying monsters are the ones that mirror ourselves.

CHAPTER 2

THE UNDEAD

The shuffling of dragging feet follows you as you clamber on all fours. The groaning increases in volume as the unnatural forces that haunt your every move begin to gain ground. You slip, your muscles fail you and all logic dissolves from your brain. They're slow, but you're scared, and helpless. And soon to become a meal for the walking dead: soulless killing machines that crave flesh and feel no pain. You're outnumbered, they keep coming... and it all ends in a flurry of red and black. You've become another victim of the relentless undead, and now you are cursed with them, to walk the earth for evermore in a quest to satisfy your insatiable hunger...

Zombie

Zombie

Common Strengths	: Resistance to physical damage, unnatural strength, herd mentality.
Common Weaknesses	: Trauma to the brain, incineration, decapitation, often slow and lumbering.

Easily one of the most common and popular monsters of the twentieth and twenty-first centuries, the classic zombie is usually a sign of a ruination of the world. They can come from dark incantations, viruses or voodoo practices, but their concept is more or less the same: the dead are made living once again, with a lack of morals or societal boundaries, and a desperate need to kill and to feed off the flesh of the living. What is it about these lumbering, rotting corpses that has made them a staple of horror for over half a century?

VOODOO ORIGINS...

Voodoo Zombies

Created by	: Garnett Weston
Appearances	: *White Zombie* (1932)

With the release of Victor Halperin's *White Zombie* in 1932, cinema's infatuation with the undead truly began. Starring Bela Lugosi as 'Murder' Legendre, it deals with a voodoo master from Haiti who creates and commands zombies. Using a poison and his insidious ways, Murder keeps zombies as slave-like companions, and they are easily led and instructed by the cruel hypnotist. While it doesn't reach the genuine terror of later movies in the zombie movie annals, it's still an original film that once again shows Lugosi's versatility and draw as an intimidating and eerie leading man.

Above: White
Zombie – © United
Artists

Right: I Walked
With a Zombie –
© RKO Radio
Pictures

The 1943 movie *I Walked With a Zombie* furthered these voodoo machinations of the genre, seeing a nurse treating a patient on a Caribbean island. Here, she makes disturbing observations of voodoo practices and citizens with unknown 'illnesses'. It soon becomes clear that not all is right on the island paradise, and things take a turn for the worse when nurse Betsy Connell (Frances Dee) discovers the chilling truth about the patient she was sent to treat, and how the community has succumbed to the dangers of voodoo rituals. The focus in this movie is on wide-eyed tension, the 'zombies' being unnerving for their unfeeling, non-reactive ways. Rather than being the flesh-eating trope that was soon to become the norm, the zombies in this film quite literally earn their title. The movie has become renowned for its unsettling atmosphere, a foreboding tone that constantly hints at the paranormal and cruel actions bubbling beneath the surface.

BEYOND THE GRAVE...

Resurrected Bodies

Created by : Ed Wood
Appearances : *Plan 9 from Outer Space* (1957)

The 1959 Ed Wood-directed cult classic, *Plan 9 From Outer Space*, saw the deceased on Earth becoming resurrected by alien beings in an attempt to prove their existence to humans and put an end to earthlings' self-destructive ways. While equally ridiculed and lauded, the film can't be seen as anything but original in its depictions of zombies. While most of the movie is filled with unrealistic and forced dialogue, the deadly, lumbering creatures that are risen are admittedly intimidating. Maila Nurmi (here going by her well-known screen name, Vampira) gives a wide-eyed, almost robotic performance as one of the unfortunately resurrected. The few zombies seen on screen throughout

Plan 9 From Outer Space – © *Valiant Pictures*

THE ULTIMATE BOOK OF MOVIE MONSTERS

the movie are mostly aimless and can be found meandering about the film's fog-covered cemetery sets.

Again, unlike later, more traditional, depictions of the undead, these creatures simply robotically carry out the will of The Ruler (John Breckinridge), Eros (Dudley Manlove) and Tanna (Joanna Lee), the main invaders responsible for the chaos on Earth. Unsurprisingly a cult classic, the movie retains B-movie merits to this day, and the zombies, equally hilarious and original, are a large part of its enduring popularity.

RISE OF THE MODERN ZOMBIE...

The Living Dead

Created by   : George A. Romero

Appearances : *Night of the Living Dead* (1968 and 1990), *Dawn of the Dead* (1978 and 2004), *Day of the Dead* (1985 and 2008) *Day of the Dead: Bloodline* (2018), *Land of the Dead* (2005), *Diary of the Dead* (2007), *Survival of the Dead* (2009), *Empire of the Dead* (2013 – Comic), *Road of the Dead: Highway to Hell* (2019 – Comic), *The Living Dead* (2020 – Novel), *Rise of the Living Dead* (2020 – Comic)

In one of the most influential movies of the twentieth century, director George A. Romero brought arguably the most classic and enduring depiction of zombies to cinema with his film *Night of the Living Dead* (1968). In it, a farmhouse is overrun by 'ghouls', re-animated corpses that seek living flesh for sustenance. Throughout the movie, radio reports reveal to the main characters that cannibalistic murders are taking place across America, and that the corpses could possibly be coming to life due to excess radiation from a launched space probe.

The lead character, Ben, and many others fight for their lives throughout the movie, using what would become time-tested methods of defeating the undead in the countless movies that followed.

Night of the Living Dead is relentless in its depiction of the undead, creating a claustrophobic, unsettling atmosphere that permeates every frame. It can't be stressed enough how Romero's original, and the five official sequels that followed, influenced so many aspects of the zombie movie genre. Because of its public domain status, the movie is easily attainable, and as such saw a number of 'unofficial' sequels and homages produced in the decades after its release.

After Romero's official follow-up, *Dawn of the Dead*, was released to critical acclaim in 1978, Italian director Lucio Fulci helmed a zombie movie called *Zombi 2*. As *Dawn of the Dead* had been released in Italy under the title *Zombi*, Fulci's new film acted as an unofficial sequel, seeking to bring the original cinematic characteristics of the undead to film. Like *White Zombie* and *I Walked with a Zombie*, voodoo plays its part in the resurrection of the violent creatures seen in *Zombi 2*. Notorious for its shockingly graphic violence (including the infamous eye-gouge scene) as well as its deceptive soundtrack – one that can lull viewers into a false sense of security with its tropical and sometimes pleasant tunes – *Zombi 2* saw more brutality at the hands of the undead as they claim victims on a Caribbean island.

Night of the Living Dead – © *Continental Distributing*

THE ULTIMATE BOOK OF MOVIE MONSTERS

Zombi 2 – © *Variety Film*

BRAAAIIIIINSSS...

Living Dead

Created by : Dan O'Bannon

Appearances : *The Return of the Living Dead* (1985), *Return of the Living Dead Part II* (1988), *Return of the Living Dead III* (1993), *Return of the Living Dead: Necropolis* (2005), *Return of the Living Dead: Rave to the Grave* (2005)

Along with Romero's official sequels, a more comic offshoot came about in 1985 in the form of *The Return of the Living Dead*. After John Russo and George Romero completed work on *Night of the Living Dead*, Russo kept the rights to titles containing *Living Dead*, and went about producing his own series of movies

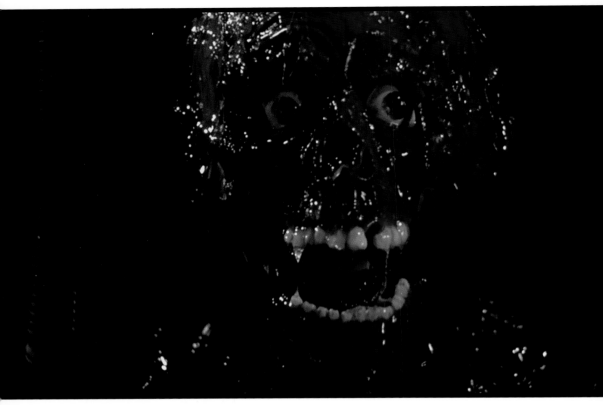

The Return of the Living Dead – © *Orion Pictures*

in a separate continuity to the films Romero would go on to create. In the 1985 comedy-horror, written and directed by Dan O'Bannon, audiences were again given a fresh take on the zombie lore, the creatures altering their need for human flesh and instead being imbued with a desire for brains.

The campy horror on show in this '80s punk-aesthetic chunk of zombie action proved to have massive appeal, becoming a box office and critical hit. Audiences and critics responded well to the more comical take on zombie flicks, with the iconic 'BRAAAIIINNSSS!!' line being used in countless other pieces of media, in stories both serious and rife with parody. The personality spewing from O'Bannon's film meant that it, and its comedic, lumbering undead ran alongside Romero's series with little negative impact on either. The practical effects and buckets of gore meant that *The Return of the Living Dead* clicked with horror fans for its over-the-top violence as much as its comedic value.

I KICK ASS FOR THE LORD!...

Zombies

Created by : Peter Jackson, Fran Walsh and Stephen Sinclair
Appearances : *Braindead* (1992 – known as *Dead Alive* in the US)

While he is now known for his two fantasy trilogies, *The Lord of the Rings* and *The Hobbit*, New Zealand director Peter Jackson started his career with riotous dark comedy and horror films such as *Bad Taste*, *Meet the Feebles* and the ultra-gory *Braindead* (1992).

Braindead is a rollercoaster of hilarity, violence and ridiculousness. Set in Wellington, it sees Lionel defending himself against a zombie onslaught after his mother is bitten by a rat-like monkey creature and transforms into a walking corpse, apparently dying multiple times throughout the film and subsequently starting a chain of infections that rocks Lionel's

Lionel (Timothy Balme) in Braindead – © Oro Films

world. He tries his best to cover up a number of zombified corpses but as the gravity of the infection sets in, his love-life hangs in the balance, and he seeks to offset the rapidly spreading undead hordes.

The movie is full of darkly-humorous moments, usually to do with gross-out close-ups and copious amounts of pus and blood. The final act of the movie sees a party in Lionel's mansion go horribly wrong, and the ensuing bloodbath is sure to keep gore-hounds happy. The infamous lawnmower scene contains arguably the most ludicrous and over-the-top bloodshed seen on film since *The Evil Dead*. Marrying genuine, laugh-out-loud moments with visceral and practical gore makes *Braindead* a must-see zombie flick, one that would see countless revisits once Peter Jackson gained Hollywood notoriety.

JOIN US...

The Evil Dead/Deadites/Kandarian Demons

Created by : Sam Raimi

Appearances : *The Evil Dead* (1981), *Evil Dead II* (1987), *Army of Darkness* (1993), *Evil Dead* (2013), *Evil Dead Rise* (2022), *Ash vs. Evil Dead* (2015–2018, TV series), *Army of Darkness* (comic series), *The Evil Dead* (comic series), *Evil Dead* (long-running video game series)

The undead present in Sam Raimi's horror masterpiece *The Evil Dead* (1981) and its sequels take on a demonic form in contrast to the brainless corpses of other zombie-focused films. The 'deadites', as they became known, are living hosts under demonic possession.

When a group of five friends (including series hero Ash Williams, played by B-movie veteran Bruce Campbell) take a vacation in a cabin in the woods, they unknowingly unleash evil entities from a cursed book of pure evil: the *Necronomicon Ex-Mortis*. What follows is an absolute nightmare brought to

The Evil Dead – © *New Line Cinema*

life, as the young adults fall victim to possession in an unholy onslaught of mimicry, torture and brutal, gory deaths.

The deadites show no remorse in their attacks on the living. They are mischievous, violent and absent of all sympathy. Imbuing the host body with inhuman strength, sadistically violent tendencies and emotionally abusive manipulation, the deadites revel in torturing, possessing and murdering their victims, feeding the *Necronomicon*'s need for chaos and bloodshed.

Ash remains to stand against them, and through his living nightmare he learns to defend himself and defeat his own friends through grisly dismemberment. Armed with a chainsaw and a double-barrelled shotgun, affectionately referred to as a 'boomstick', he fights a seemingly unending battle from the fateful cabin in the woods , to medieval times and back again, the deadite threat even following him into his 50s in the follow-up TV series *Ash vs. Evil Dead* (2015–2018). After the original movie, the series steered more into a slapstick comedy-horror hybrid, maintaining the gratuitous violence but putting a more comedic slant on the bloodshed and dialogue.

In the 2013 reboot, *Evil Dead*, the pure horror tone of the original 1981 movie came back into play. Here, the deadites are once again sadistic, twisted

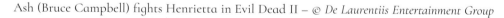

Ash (Bruce Campbell) fights Henrietta in Evil Dead II – © *De Laurentiis Entertainment Group*

Mia (Jane Levy) while possessed in Evil Dead (2013) – © *Sony Pictures Releasing*

creatures, unreservedly decimating the bodies of those they possess in order to shock and terrify their victims. A new group visits the iconic cabin in order to help main character Mia drop a drug habit and go cold turkey in a safe environment. It's not long before they are fighting for their very souls in an attempt to escape and stop the resurrection of a merciless entity. The terror continues in a fifth installment, *Evil Dead Rise*, directed by Lee Cronin, who helmed *The Hole in the Ground*. Some of cinema's most relentless and terrifying monsters, the deadites continue to disgust and shock to this day.

A possessed Olivia (Jessica Lucas) mutilates herself in Evil Dead (2013) – © *Sony Pictures Releasing*

SOLVE THE PUZZLE...

Cenobites

Created by : Clive Barker

Appearances : *Hellraiser* (1987), *Hellbound: Hellraiser II* (1988), *Hellraiser III: Hell on Earth* (1992), *Hellraiser: Bloodline* (1996), *Hellraiser: Inferno* (2000), *Hellraiser: Hellseeker* (2002), *Hellraiser: Deader* (2005), *Hellraiser: Hellworld* (2005), *Hellraiser: Revelations* (2011), *Hellraiser: Judgement* (2018)

The eternal debauchery of the Cenobites brings both pain and pleasure to those they cross paths with. These inter-dimensional beings, stars of the *Hellraiser* series and led by the nightmareish 'Pinhead', are unfeeling in their ways, guided by no moral compass, but rather by their innate desires for carnal pleasures.

Summoned from their own hellish dominion by the solving of a cube-shaped puzzle box, the Cenobites are horrific and warped beings, physically exaggerated

Cenobites in Hellraiser *– © Entertainment Film Distributors*

and disfigured to a terrifying degree. The leader, Pinhead, is a black-eyed, humanoid pin-cushion, with a grid-like face and a devilish, domineering voice. He leads the group with an unnerving confidence, an almost charming façade that forgoes his seedy intentions. Lusting for torture and bloodshed, Pinhead would be the face of the Cenobites throughout the series of hugely popular horror movies, played for the majority by Doug Bradley, who gives a breathtaking performance that is sure to raise as many hairs as it does hell.

His accomplices fare no better in the looks department. The eyeless demon, Chatterer, is a twisted creature, all teeth and creased skin, and his maw with its gruesome, bloodied teeth makes him almost as visually formidable as his master. While he may not have the strength of wordplay that Pinhead so readily commands, Chatterer is a mostly silent antagonist, physically powerful and intimidating with his mere presence and those hideous, chattering teeth.

Butterball is a multi-chinned, bulbous humanoid, who dons a thick pair of sunglasses to hide his eyes, which have been sown shut. Like Chatterer, he is a physically imposing demon, preferring to remain silent as Pinhead deals with the whims, desires and fates of those unlucky enough to complete the puzzle box.

The fan-named 'Deepthroat', a female Cenobite with a disgustingly disfigured and exposed throat, roams with her three companions, and her deep-set, harrowing eyes intimidate and intrigue in equal measure. She inhabits Labyrinth with her cohorts and, like them, is clad in an elaborate leather outfit. The Cenobite costumes allude to the 'pleasure' side of their ventures, while their more obvious, grotesquely twisted physical features betray their penchant for pain and torture.

Throughout the 10-movie series, many more Cenobites were introduced, such as a demon with CDs jutting from his head, and a former cameraman who now has a camera embedded in his skull in place of one of his eyes.

The inspired and disturbing design of the Cenobites, born from director Clive Barker's unique vision (the series is based on Barker's novella *The Hellbound Heart*), are the epitome of morbidly intriguing monsters. While they are undeniably evil and technically hideous to look at, there is a demand from fans of this franchise to see more, as evidenced by the amount of movies produced, as well as the expansion of the series into comics which deepen the mythology and increase the numbers of Pinhead's blasphemous gang.

STAYING ALIVE IS AS GOOD AS IT GETS...

Infected

Created by : Alex Garland

Appearances : *28 Days Later* (2002), *28 Weeks Later* (2007), *28 Days Later: The Aftermath* (2007 – comic book), *28 Days Later* (2009 – 2011 – comic book series)

Acclaimed director Danny Boyle brought the terrifying infected of *28 Days Later* to screens in 2002. Far removed from the slow and lumbering stereotypical zombies of past movies in the genre, *28 Days Later* and its sequel, *28 Weeks Later*, both include rabid and frantic infected humans, who quickly become crazed and bloodthirsty upon contracting a terrifying virus.

Starring Cillian Murphy and Naomie Harris, the movie is unique in the zombie landscape. By bucking the stereotypes of resurrected deceased or infected, brain-eating ghouls terrorising the American countryside and major cities, *28 Days Later* brings the terror to an abandoned London, creating a unique and lonely atmosphere that keeps the threat real and unpredictable. With a distinct indie feel, the movie roots itself in realism thanks to intriguing character drama and a fantastic and believable cast. These immersive performances coupled with a completely original take on the zombie stereotype meant that the series brought a renewed interest in media concerning zombies, be it in literature, film, television or video games.

Infection can come from any number of avenues, and if any blood or fluid of an infected is ingested by a living creature, it will rapidly become crazed and murderous, relentlessly hunting anything living in sight. Gone is the hours or days-long conversion of humans to brainless shufflers. Instead, *28 Days Later* sees real, interesting characters having to quickly come to terms with their friends' loss of humanity, and emotions are high as the tragedies pile up.

The feral and relentless infected, notable for their incredible speed – in contrast to the shuffling, decaying creatures of the George A. Romero classics – make for

28 Days Later –
© Fox Searchlight Pictures

seat-gripping cinema, and the vicious horror of the 28 series has cemented the horrifying creatures as memorable and pioneering movie monsters.

MOTHER NATURE IS
A SERIAL KILLER...

Zombies

Created by : Max Brooks

Appearances : *World War Z: An Oral History of the Zombie War* (2006 – Novel), *World War Z* (2013), *World War Z* (2013 & 2019 – video games)

World War Z (2013), based on the novel by Max Brooks (son of comedic legend Mel Brooks), depicted the undead with a terrifying ferocity. Known for its pulse-pounding action and overwhelming swarms of zombies, the movie sees

A horde of zombies in World War Z *– © Paramount Pictures*

swathes of the relentless creatures ravage the Earth, and follows Gerry Lane (Brad Pitt) as he attempts to navigate the deadly apocalyptic scenario in order to aid in the search for a vaccine to end the zombie plague.

It has a gripping opening scene that shows how quickly the world can come to its knees in the face of a deadly plague, and a standout scene which serves to hit home just how determined these monsters are to reach their prey. The infected are seen using each other as leverage, creating a wall of zombies, similar to the ladder formation ants take to reach higher spaces. The herd mentality is consistent with many other forms of zombie media, and the monsters are attracted by loud noises and the sight of uninfected people.

Rather than consume the flesh of the living, the zombies in *World War Z* are driven to spread the disease as quickly as possible. Once bitten, infection is rapid, almost instantaneous, and this biological reaction leads to many major cities falling to the hordes in a short amount of time. Drawn to healthy, living flesh, the infected have been known to ignore people who are incapacitated or in ill health or stricken by injury. This makes it seem as though they choose the optimum prey so as to spread infection more rapidly – an absolutely terrifying prospect that sees more of the herd mentality inherent in these creatures come to the forefront.

The global adventure is a thrilling race against time, for family and the salvation of humanity. Time is of the essence when it comes to the ferocious infected of this unique movie.

THE ULTIMATE BOOK OF MOVIE MONSTERS

JUST R...

Zombies & Boneys

Created by : Isaac Marion
Appearances : *Warm Bodies* (2010 – novel), *Warm Bodies* (2013)

Warm Bodies (2013), based on the novel of the same name by Isaac Marion, stands apart from genre conventions by offering a heartwarming (literally) look into the humanity that remains when someone is touched by monstrosity. During an undead apocalypse, a zombie known as R is stuck in a rut of repetitive feeding and roaming, sating his need for brains but mostly going through the motions. While satisfying his hunger he comes to know Julie, and the two slowly learn about each other as their affinity grows.

As Julie shows R respect, kindness and, eventually, love, he miraculously begins a gradual reversal of his condition. As his body warms to Julie's

Julie (Teresa Palmer) and R (Nicholas Hoult) in Warm Bodies *– © Summit Entertainment*

romance, R begins to regain his human traits. While the story is endearing and exciting, the threat of misunderstanding looms over their relationship, as most still believe R to be a heartless creature that murders without remorse. As they attempt to convince Julie's colonel father of R's returning humanity, they must also contend with 'Boneys', fully transformed undead who have lost all traces of their humanity and shed their skin.

R fights to protect Julie despite her recurring reluctance to trust him due to his past actions. R's persistence as an oncoming human mirrors his determination as a zombie to find and devour his much-needed sustenance. With a plethora of challenges facing him, both physical and emotional, R is one of the most well-rounded and sympathetic 'monsters' to be seen on film in recent years.

The zombie genre has moved from its voodoo origins to the more common, shuffling, flesh-eating creatures most prominent in the genre. Movies like *28 Days Later* and the Spanish found-footage series, *REC*, brought terrifying speed and agility to the infected. In recent times, films like *Warm Bodies* and the Korean white-knuckle ride *Train to Busan* (2016) have aimed to give undead flicks a more weighty, emotional and human slant. While an over-saturation in all forms of entertainment has seen the popularity of zombies slightly wane, history dictates that they will emerge from the grave again in some form of undead renaissance, to shuffle and roam about the Earth, long after we are all gone...

CHAPTER 3

COLOSSAL BEASTS

A thunderous quake awakens you from a deep sleep. Another follows. It's getting louder, closer. It must be off the Richter scale. You peer through your window to see the crowds gathering in the city streets below. The surrounding buildings begin to crumble and your lights go out. Each pulse of the earth sends a multitude of objects crashing about your apartment. Shards of glass leave gashes across your body as you tumble forwards, through the window and out into the street. Your head is fuzzy, your arm is broken. Numb with pain but high on adrenaline, you hear a passer-by ask if you're ok. And then you hear the screams. The thunderous quakes are now piercing the air and quickly making those screams inaudible. Your body gets tossed about the concrete and through blurry eyes you see the bodies torn and mangled beneath debris. The quaking stops, but your head continues to thump. Your raise your head to see it... A beast that stretches to the very clouds themselves. Piercing black eyes the size of

Godzilla – © Toho

wrecking balls meet yours. A slimy tentacle grasps your midriff as you feel all of your ribs crack and implode. The last thing you see is the terrifying vision of razor-sharp teeth, each one bigger than your body. Your numbness becomes the most excruciating pain, until you can feel no more...

Godzilla

Common Strengths	: Atomic heat beam, rapid underwater traversal, nuclear regeneration, electromagnetic shield.
Common Weaknesses	: (Occasionally) Electric attacks, extreme cold, blunt force from a more powerful being.

Few monsters instill the type of existential fear that gargantuan, marauding beasts do. When we see them on film, the characters – and to an extent, the audience – feel helpless. For decades, the cities of Earth have been terrorised by the battles and rampages of countless monsters the size of skyscrapers: abominations that can level entire blocks with one step.

KING OF THE MONSTERS...

Gojira (Godzilla)

Created by	: Tomoyuki Tanaka, Ishirō Honda, Eiji Tsubaraya
Appearances	: *Godzilla* (Toho series), *Godzilla* (1998), *Godzilla* (Legendary's MonsterVerse series)

Disaster movies, superhero movies and horror movies have all seen their share of colossal beasts, but when thinking of creatures that crack the clouds with their might, there is arguably no single behemoth more recognised than the

Godzilla (2014) – © Warner Bros. Pictures

mighty Godzilla. The monster put the kaiju (or, 'Strange Beast') genre on the map, and its popularity has only grown since.

Rightly labelled the King of the Monsters, this Japanese cinematic icon has been blasting and destroying for both the safety and destruction of the human race since the 1950s. The towering lizard made his debut in the original 1954 classic, *Godzilla*, directed by Ishirō Honda. The sea-dwelling dinosaur began a half-century rampage that continues to this day. Initially created as a metaphor for the bombings of Hiroshima and Nagasaki, Godzilla and his nuclear might proved a bane and a boon for the citizens of Tokyo and other cities around the world. While he primarily caused a ruckus with his gargantuan size and careless tendencies towards demolition, the movie series began to throw other beasts into the mix in opposition to the dangerous lizard. From partial friends like the elusive and dream-like Mothra, to mortal enemies like the mighty, three-headed dragon King Ghidorah, the creature known as Godzilla has used Earth as his battleground for over 60 years.

While the tone of the movies and origins of the creature changed throughout the 36 movies featuring the King of the Monsters, many of his characteristics and powers have remained in the majority. As he is said to have been roused and charged by nuclear power, he can shoot an atomic ray from his gaping maw, an ability which has obliterated building and beast alike. His mammoth tail has been used to sweep unsuspecting creatures throughout his battles, and his ability to traverse the world using the oceans meant that his adventures could be world-spanning with relative ease.

The effects that have brought this ancient beast to the screen have varied with the passage of time. While many of the early movies featured agile actors in full body suits, duking it out over miniature sets to give a sense of scale to the proceedings, later movies such as Roland Emmerich's tonally-light 1998 effort starring Matthew Broderick, and the more recent MonsterVerse movies (also containing the mighty Kong in the same continuity), saw Godzilla rendered using high-quality computer-generated animation. While the movies of the '50s up to the '70s have a massive charm and appeal for their multitude of creatures and practical sets and choreography, the more recent Hollywood efforts have helped to realise high-quality battles with iconic series monsters. In 2019's *Godzilla: King of the Monsters,* many well-known monsters from Toho – the Japanese Production company behind dozens of monster movies – are brought to big-budget life in a globe-trotting battle that sees these terrifying god-like beings vying for supremacy as humanity falls by the wayside.

Godzilla is an absolute icon of cinema, and is versatile in his appeal, ranging from an all-out hero who prevents the destruction of the Earth to a terrifying harbinger of doom, destroying entire cities and wrecking life on our planet with his insurmountable nuclear might. Being as powerful as the iconic kaiju is, it made sense for his enemies to come equipped with their own monstrous abilities so as to have a fighting chance against the ocean-dwelling lizard king.

QUEEN OF THE MONSTERS...

Mothra

Created by : Shinichiro Nakamura, Yoshie Hotta, Takehiko Fukanaga
Appearances : Toho Monster movies, Legendary's MonsterVerse series

Mothra is second only to Godzilla in the kaiju hierarchy, and the massive, celestial moth has played a key role throughout the storied history of Japanese monsters. Like Godzilla, Mothra has gone through many incarnations,

Mothra – © Toho

occasionally seen as destructive towards humanity due to her colossal size, but more memorably she is seen as a sort of otherworldly guardian to humanity. She has also been seen to aid Godzilla and other monsters in their battles against some of the more vicious creatures of the franchise.

She first appeared in the 1961 film, *Mothra*. Dwelling on and guarding Infant Island, Mothra is immortal, in that she is always reborn from a new egg, even if she is defeated. As such, it makes her a mighty guardian and strong opposition to the more insidious monsters from the *Godzilla* franchise. She is often accompanied by two miniature beings, the Shobijin, who speak on her behalf. With a life cycle similar to a common moth, she hatches from her egg in larval caterpillar form, before becoming her fully-grown, powerful self, with impressive, colourful wings and massive, keen eyes.

While her protective sensibilities are more common in the series, she has come into conflict with Godzilla on a few occasions. The black moth, Battra, teamed with Mothra to neutralise the King of the Monsters and prevent a meteor from crashing into Earth.

Mothra in Godzilla: King of the Monsters – © Warner Bros. Pictures

THE ULTIMATE BOOK OF MOVIE MONSTERS

Conversely, she next warned of the coming of SpaceGodzilla, a cosmic entity said to have been formed when some of Godzilla's organic matter passed through a black hole.

In *Godzilla: King of the Monsters* from 2019, Mothra appears, much larger than before but still with her cosmic, god-like powers, and she aids Godzilla later in the movie as he battles for supremacy against the mighty King Ghidorah.

THE THREE-HEADED MONSTER...

King Ghidorah

Created by : Tomoyuki Tanaka
Appearances : Toho's Monster series, Legendary's MonsterVerse series

King Ghidorah, or Monster Zero, is an extra-terrestrial terror and the arch enemy of Godzilla. A dragon-like monster, he has three heads with long necks, outstretched wings and two tails. Usually, he is seen as equal or slightly bigger in size than Godzilla. While his origins vary depending on the era of Godzilla movies, he is most commonly a planet-ravaging menace. He makes his way across galaxies conquering planets with his absolute might.

King Ghidorah in Godzilla: King of the Monsters *– © Warner Bros. Pictures*

He has come to blows with Godzilla on many occasions, fighting tooth and claw with the King in order to assert his dominance. He's also known to cause catastrophic damage and death to the human race in the process. Monster Zero doesn't worry about the world, but how much fun he has in its decimation.

He is equipped with powerful gravity beams which can cut through flesh and buildings with ease, causing absolute devastation for those unfortunate enough to incur his wrath. He can also protect himself with an energy shield during onslaughts, and can blast hurricane winds from his massive wings.

His three heads communicate telepathically, as well as receive orders from outside his own body. In *King of the Monsters*, Monarch (a company in charge of researching and controlling kaiju threats) theorises that Ghidorah is an Alpha Titan, just as Godzilla is, and they will stop at nothing to exterminate each other in order to be crowned King. When humanity is trapped in the cross-fire, what will be the ultimate cost of being pawns in the battleground of these gargantuan, eternal beasts?

THE PTERANODON...

Rodan

Created by   : Ken Kuronuma

Appearances : Toho's Monster series, Legendary's MonsterVerse series

---

Rodan, a Pteranodon beast, was initially seen as an enemy of Godzilla, taunting him and obsessing over their battles. As the eras went on, specifically when he and Godzilla witnessed Mothra trying to battle Ghidorah on her own, Rodan joined forces with Godzilla to aid in the space terror's defeat. Since then, Rodan is normally an ally of Godzilla, helping him to defeat enemy monsters like Ghidorah and MechaGodzilla.

His bird-like form is even more dinosaur in its appearance than Godzilla, and this makes sense, as one of the earliest origins for this classic creature

Rodan in Godzilla: King of the Monsters *– © Warner Bros. Pictures*

was his survival of the extinction event that killed off the dinosaurs. Being irradiated over millions of years meant that Rodan grew to his colossal size, and was imbued with devastating powers. He has been known to breathe fire to attack foes and the environment. When weakened, some versions of Rodan can absorb life from around him, such as animals and plants, in order to regain his strength. He is also able to fly at tremendous speeds.

Rodan is involved in the global battle of *Godzilla: King of the Monsters*, where he takes part in the fight that mainly involves Ghidorah and Godzilla. Rodan should never be counted out however, and this enduring Toho monster is a long-time fan favourite.

THE KING OF SKULL ISLAND...

King Kong

Created by   : Edgar Wallace, Merian C. Cooper
Appearances : RKO Radio series, *King Kong* (2005), Legendary's MonsterVerse series

Preceding the debut of Godzilla was the elusive Kong. Roaring to life in the 1933 original (whose story was remade in both 1976 and 2005), the story of the massive ape who dwells on the wild and unexplored Skull Island has become an iconic part of film history. Setting audience's imaginations on fire with its exotic setting, stellar special effects and heart-wrenching storyline, the sympathy-driven tale sees King Kong act as a protector and suitor to a human woman, Ann Darrow, all the while dealing with a mix of fascination and hostility at the hands of his captors.

Like Godzilla, King Kong has been placed head-to-head with many deadly creatures and, using his mighty strength and furious rage, has bested his share of hideous monsters in the nearly 90 years since he first appeared on screen. While he has typically scrapped with the exotic mutations that dwell on his home island – specifically in Peter Jackson's King Kong in 2005 and the MonsterVerse entry Kong: Skull Island in 2017 – he has also come to blows with the King of the Monsters on more than one occasion. Knowing the draw for both Japanese and American audiences, filmmakers brought the two behemoths together in 1962's *King Kong vs. Godzilla* and 2021's *Godzilla vs. Kong*. The former was the first time that both monsters appeared in full colour, and the movies both deliver on their promise of the fan service spectacle

King Kong – © *Radio Pictures*

Kong: Skull Island – © *Warner Bros. Pictures*

that comes with a clash of two Kings with completely ludicrous strength and mind-bending power.

More than an environmental menace, Kong is notable for his emotional responses to those around him, both in his gentle relationship to Ann Darrow and his unbridled fury at the violent and torturous tendencies of those who invaded his home and stole his freedom. The sympathy brought from audiences for this monster gives an emotional weight to the battles he faces. As such, the character has been syndicated into several TV series, as his demeanour and physicality lends itself well to both children's television and adventure in general.

FROM THE DEPTHS...

The Beast from 20,000 Fathoms

Created by : Ray Bradbury, Ray Harryhausen
Appearances : *The Beast from 20,000 Fathoms* (1953)

A 'massive' inspiration for Godzilla was *The Beast from 20,000 Fathoms* (1953). This ocean-dwelling lizard, brought to life with then-revolutionary special effects, is a brutal force of nature. Devoid of all compassion, it wreaks pure destruction on everything in its path. Devouring the people it sees and revelling in the carnage of wrecked vehicles and buildings, the powerful creature bears a formidable ridged body, a massive set of nasty teeth and a lengthy, muscular tail that makes short work of even the most stable structures. The special effects and stop-motion legend Ray Harryhausen brought his wonderful work to the creature, giving it an organic and original feel.

With its strong limbs and furrowed brow, the beast is menacing, and, unlike many movie monsters from the earlier decades of the century, it's not overly tame by today's standards. This is full-on monster movie mayhem, and there's little respite for the citizens as the massive monster smashes all in its path. The destruction of practical sets gives the beast's actions real impact, a weighty form in its gripping stop-motion obliteration that makes its rampage eerily realistic and full of cinematic flair.

The Beast from 20,000 Fathoms – © *Warner Bros. Pictures*

While it's nowhere near the size of some of the kaiju or towering abominations that followed, it nevertheless set a standard for disaster and monster movies for decades after, and it's one that is still the template for countless imitators today.

A VERY BIG PROBLEM...

Nancy, the 50 Foot Woman

Created by : Mark Hanna
Appearances : *Attack of the 50 Foot Woman* (1958), *Attack of the 50 Ft. Woman* (1993)

Nancy feels like she has it tough. An uncertain life and future with her husband has her in the depths of despair. As she's driving home one night, she bears witness to what appears to be an unidentified flying object. Against her best instincts, she decides to investigate. But what she finds there will change her life forever.

As far removed as possible from the stomping, careless beasts of other classic monster movies, *Attack of the 50 Foot Woman* is a truly human monster story. What if we found *we* had become the monster, overnight?

Nancy Archer (Allison Hayes) in Attack of the 50 Foot Woman – @ *Allied Artists Pictures Corporation*

After her encounter with the spaceship, Nancy begins to experience some curious changes. As parts of her anatomy begin to enlarge, she suspects the extra-terrestrial encounter has left her with some highly unwanted side-effects. Frightening those once close to her with her gargantuan form, she becomes the talk of the town, for all the wrong reasons.

The most simple movements become troublesome, as Nancy smashes all about her with her newfound strength and size. Yet, as worried as she is by the initial shock, she begins to feel empowered by her physical advantages, and it doesn't take too long for her to exact forms of revenge on those who wronged her when she was just regular old Nancy.

With a combination of miniature sets to enhance Nancy's size, and comical, massive prosthetic limbs protruding from the sides of the frame, this entirely unique 'monster' concept comes to life in a way that somehow manages to honour its name and make it feel schlocky, yet somehow touch on a real and relatable story that should be familiar to anyone who has ever felt downtrodden when it comes to respect and to life's ups and downs.

IT JUST POPPED IN THERE...

The Stay-Puft Marshmallow Man

Created by   : Dan Aykroyd and Harold Ramis
Appearances : *Ghostbusters* (1984), *Ghostbusters II* (1989), *The Real Ghostbusters* (1986–1991 animated series), *Ghostbusters: The Video Game* (2009)

While he may be supernatural in origin, the Stay-Puft Marshmallow Man has to be included alongside other giant movie monsters for his iconic appearance in the original *Ghostbusters* (1984).

As Ray, Winston, Egon and Peter attempt to save New York from the other-worldly rift created by the demonic Sumerian god, Gozer, the powerful entity disappears from sight and offers the heroes a choice. It will soon return

The Stay-Puft Marshmallow Man in Ghostbusters *– © Colombia Pictures*

to destroy the city, but the Ghostbusters are given the choice of what form the demon-god will take.

While the others look confused, Ray Stantz looks terrified. Having thought of an in-universe mascot for marshmallows, Ray believed he had saved the team trouble by choosing something that is mostly harmless.

But this rendition of the Marshmallow Man is over 100 feet tall, and his booming footsteps can be heard across New York. His chubby face, once permanently fixed into a smile, now bears an angry frown as he stomps about the streets, watching panicked civilians scurry about his humongous, squidgy feet.

Turning a loveable mascot, who bears more than a striking resemblance to the Michelin Man, into a gargantuan, walking disaster is a stroke of genius that could only happen in *Ghostbusters*. Stay-Puft would go on to reappear in the cartoon series *The Real Ghostbusters*, *Ghostbusters: The Video Game* (which acts as a sequel to *Ghostbusters II*), and *Ghostbusters: Afterlife*, in "Mini-Puft" form.

IT'S ALIVE... IT'S HUGE...

The Cloverfield Monster

Created by : J.J. Abrams and Neville Page

Appearances : *Cloverfield* (2008), *The Cloverfield Paradox* (2018), *Cloverfield/Kishin* (2008 – manga comic book)

Seeking to bring a classic American monster to the cinematic landscape, producer J.J. Abrams developed a beast to rival Toho's mighty Godzilla. In 2007, cryptic movie trailers with no title attached alluded to attacks on New York City by an unseen and presumably gigantic force. Combined with an alternate reality online advertising campaign complete with news snippets and cryptic puzzles, the mystery built up over months, eventually revealing itself to be promotion for a found-footage monster movie called *Cloverfield*.

In *Cloverfield*, a farewell party in New York is suddenly interrupted by massive tremors and power outages. The cause of this destruction is slowly revealed to be a colossal beast that has risen from the depths of the ocean and is wreaking

The Cloverfield Monster – © *Paramount Pictures*

havoc among the skyscrapers of the Big Apple. Designed by legendary creature artist Neville Page, the *Cloverfield* monster is a gangly, towering behemoth, with pure-black eyes, a maw of razor-sharp teeth and long, powerful limbs that destroy all around it with ease.

Its near-impenetrable skin means the army forces called in to defend the city stand little chance against the creature. Adding to the terror of the beast's attack, it also sheds small, lighting-quick creatures from its body that scuttle about the city streets and relentlessly pursue civilians. Their bite causes a slow, but fatal reaction, wherein the victim's stomach eventually expands and their body bursts, causing instant death. The combination of inescapable death brought down by the towering goliath and the frantic, deadly encounters on ground level ensure that *Cloverfield* holds its own against some of the most famous and powerful kaiju from cinema's long and storied history.

While the 2008 movie gives very little background on the creature (it was fleshed out to some degree in the alternate reality campaign and in the prequel manga, *Cloverfield/Kishin*), the third movie in the franchise, *The Cloverfield Paradox* (2018), at least offers a reality-warping reason for the creature to have appeared in our universe in the first place. Likewise, *Paradox*, does something to explain the

The Cloverfield Monster – © *Paramount Pictures*

origins of the strange goings-on in the second installment in the sci-fi anthology, *10 Cloverfield Lane* (2016).

No other movie in recent years managed the feat of secrecy with such a staggering amount of information regarding a piece of entertainment than the original *Cloverfield* did. That fact that little-to-no audience members even knew what the monster looked like is a testament to how perfectly marketed and expertly revealed this franchise was. Thankfully, the imposing and destructive *Cloverfield* monster managed to live up to the hype by wreaking absolute havoc in its wake and striking pure fear into the hearts of viewers.

DRIFTING...

Kaiju

Created by : Guillermo del Toro
Appearances : *Pacific Rim* (2013), *Pacific Rim: Uprising* (2018), *Pacific Rim: The Black* (2021 – Netflix animated series), *Pacific Rim: The Video Game* (2013)

The kaiju of the *Pacific Rim* series come to blows with man-made Jaeger mechs in spectacular battles that see a duo of mentally linked pilots controlling humanity's metallic hopes against the seemingly impossible menace. Pushing full-throttle action and backed by a tragic backstory, *Pacific Rim* (2013) and its sequel are popcorn monster movies.

The kaiju have entered our world through a massive portal referred to as 'The Breach', which has opened in the Pacific Ocean. Humanity has fought for years with these mutant beasts, colossi that can ravage cities with ease. With the Jaegers, the humans have constructed metal behemoths to rival the inter-dimensional army, and what were once insurmountable foes can be taken in hand-to-hand, or rather hand-to-claw-to-horn combat. The Jaegers also come equipped with a variety of weaponry such as pulse canons, missile launchers and ludicrously sized swords. Claws and steel collide in numerous

Above: *Kaiju in Pacific Rim* – © *Warner Bros. Pictures*

Below: *Kaiju and a Jaeger doing battle* – © *Warner Bros. Pictures*

battles in the sea and on land and should provide monster movie fans with a boatload of action-packed fights to satiate their need for creature-smashing action.

The humanity of the characters shine throughout both movies, whether it's a terminal family member offering up the ultimate sacrifice for the greater good, or a returning war hero trying to redeem himself and seek vengeance for the death of his brother. With high sci-fi concepts such as monster hive-minds that offer the creatures strong reconnaissance, and neural links that allow Jaeger pilots to share their strengths and stresses, *Pacific Rim* stands on its own for bucking the trend of scurrying victims struggling to survive a wave of destruction at the hands of these massive, alien monsters.

KING vs. KING...

While they had already clashed once in the franchise with *King Kong vs. Godzilla* in 1962, the 2021 kaiju/titan mash-up *Godzilla vs. Kong* saw these two titans battle again in a special effects-laden extravaganza that was the culmination of the four-movie MonsterVerse by Legendary Pictures.

When Godzilla returns without warning after a five-year absence, ex-members of the titan expert group Monarch, and scientists from research firm Apex, struggle to understand what is causing the once-heroic creature to lash out at innocent cities. While moving Kong from his now uninhabitable home, Skull Island, the humans use this as an opportunity to try and make it to the Hollow Earth, a world inside our own that is thought to have been the birthplace of the titans.

The movie is a love letter to both franchises, mixing genuine, human emotion with rousing adventure, all wrapped up with plenty of colossal monster fighting action. No stone is left unturned in the battles between Godzilla and Kong, and the movie continually plays with viewers, flipping what we think we know on its head. Kong may seem outmatched, as all he really has going for him is agility and strength, but the film does a fantastic job of keeping the playing field even, as many no doubt assumed Godzilla would have this fight

Godzilla vs. Kong – © *Warner Bros. Pictures*

wrapped up in seconds. Fate intervenes and natural obstacles play their part in making sure no fight goes the way you may think.

Globe-trotting, inner-earth trotting and skyscraper-busting, it's hard to think that any fan of kaiju movies or monster movies in general would be disappointed at the action and emotion on show in this movie, as Adam Wingard (*The Guest, You're Next*) offers zippy direction that knows not to overstay its welcome on any given scene.

Allowing these two goliaths their own films to delve into their powers and backstory was a great way to build to this pay off, and the movie feels like an end to this era of the monster universe. We can only hope it will be the beginning of something even bigger!

Gigantic creatures make us feel helpless, and their awesome size and destructive capabilities have been the backdrop to some of the most spectacular stories ever told on film. Always a challenge for the human race, these beasts bring dread upon us like no other movie monsters.

CHAPTER 4

GHASTLY GHOULS

The bathwater is just right. After what felt like the longest shift in existence, you just want to forget about your worries, forget about unpacking and have a great night's sleep. Every muscle relaxes as you submerge yourself to the neck in the warm water, the aroma of the candles and bath salts leaving you breathing deeply. Did you drift off? The candles have burnt out. No... they were blown out? A burst of noise. The TV in your bedroom is on, at full volume. Nearly slipping to the ground you pull a towel from the rack and wrap it around yourself. Grasping the remote control with a still soaking hand you fumble for the off switch. The cacophonous news bulletin ceases and you breathe a sigh of relief. You put the remote back on the nightstand but your hand freezes afterwards. The photo of you and your partner that sits by the bed is... different. Your face has been scratched out, leaving only your partner smiling, holding hands with a faceless being. The lights in the room burst and you let out a gasp as glass falls from the ceiling. Surrounded by darkness, all you can hear is your own rapid breaths and the beating of your heart. Through the darkness, in the very corner of the room, you see something... darker. Darker than the darkness of the room, something almost... human? You slowly move closer, knowing it to be the corner lamp, framed in a deceptive way in the gloom of your bedroom. Silence. You move closer. What you thought was the lamp is breathing too, wheezing, and the silhouette of an oozing, gaping maw appears before you. The being cocks its head as it hovers before you, and you are suddenly met with two

Regan from The Exorcist – © Warner Bros. Pictures

thin, bright eyes that pull your soul into the void. It grins as your heart stops with fear, and you collapse to the soft carpet, twitching, your body white and freezing in an instant. This is its house. What were you thinking, moving in?

Regan (Possessed by Pazuzu)

Common Strengths : Contortion, emotional abuse, inhuman strength, near-omniscience

Common Weaknesses : Barely any, but can become weary of host body, letting guard down

Some ghostly or supernatural entities from the history of cinema bypass simple spectral nuisances and go directly into the realm of tangible monsters, such is their difference from floating corporeal beings typically seen in ghost stories. These fiendish ghouls cause grief and death wherever they choose to haunt, and provide movie-lovers with plenty of sleepless nights.

THE POWER OF CHRIST COMPELS YOU!...

Regan

Created by : William Peter Blatty

Appearances : *The Exorcist* (1971 – Novel), *The Exorcist* (1973), *Exorcist II: The Heretic* (1977)

William Friedkin directed the legendary adaptation of William Peter Blatty's novel, *The Exorcist*, in 1973. Often topping lists of the scariest horror movies of

Regan, possessed and contorted – © Warner Bros. Pictures

all time, the film's iconic scenes and practical effects make it a must-watch for horror movie fans. At the time of release the movie shocked audiences with its tale of devilish possession. The young girl, Regan, undergoes some of the most horrifying transformations seen on film, as her body becomes host to a demonic entity called Pazuzu, that infests her spirit and forces her to do improbable, disgusting acts.

The movie is an all-out assault on the senses, as the possessed Regan battles with a duo of priests her mother has enlisted in an act of desperation. The claustrophobic paranormal activity on show from the devil range from vulgar abuse designed to provoke and incite rage and misery, to contortions of the poor girl's body, leading to the infamous 'spider crawl' scene in which the demon climbs the staircase upside-down in an unnatural, crab-like scuttle.

It's filled with shocking, gross-out moments that are sure to have viewers' jaws agape. The crucifix scene has always been the source of much controversy, as it sees the demon denounce Jesus with some choice language, while mutilating itself below the belt with the wooden cross. Twisting heads, green vomit and the callous teasing of loved ones' fates in the afterlife are all a game to the satanic intruder, who slaps a disgusting, rotten visage on the innocent Regan.

An intense battle which seeks to question the very meaning of faith and spirituality, *The Exorcist* has always garnered attention for its extreme horror, often for being a powerful masterpiece, but occasionally for being seen as offensive to religious groups. What it is, simply, is a fantastic horror movie that stands the test of time, with stellar make-up on a remarkable monster, effective and emotional performances and direction that hits all the right beats. It doesn't hurt that the movie was scripted by Blatty, the author of the novel on which it's based. He would also go on to write and direct *The Exorcist III* (1990), which was also based on one of his own novels, *Legion*.

Some thought the R rating was too lenient for the horrible happenings on screen. There were reports of cinema-goers fainting, vomiting and in need of psychiatric help after viewings, such was the extremity of the occurrences throughout.

Those results are debatable, and certainly highly unlikely in this day and age. However, the impact of the film is undeniable, and Linda Blair's tortured performance as Regan is one of cinema's greatest triumphs – a psychological, satanic and twisted monster who seeks only to abuse and manipulate.

Father Merrin (Max von Sydow) and Regan (Linda Blair) – © Warner Bros. Pictures

TIPTOE... THROUGH THE TULIPS...

Red-faced Man

Created by : James Wan and Leigh Whannell

Appearances : *Insidious* (2011), *Insidious: Chapter 2* (2013), *Insidious: Chapter 3* (2015), *Insidious: The Last Key* (2018)

The *Insidious* series has brought some terrifying imagery and legendary jump scares since it began in 2011 with the original haunted house (haunted boy?) story. In it, young Dalton and his family are pestered by malicious spirits who are eventually discovered to be centred on Dalton himself. Through contact with a spiritual expert and medium, they discover 'The Further', a plane beyond ours that can house malevolent spirits who occasionally cross over into our world.

The film and its sequels (*Insidious: Chapter 3* and *Insidious: The Last Key* both act as prequels) delve further into this vast mythology while keeping the tension at a ridiculously high level. Their final acts resemble something of a ghost train ride, with spooks and spirits leaping from every corner, and downright odd and abstract imagery abounding.

Lipstick-faced Demon stalks Josh (Patrick Wilson) – © Sony Pictures Releasing

Arguably the most famous creature in the series is one that goes by many names. The Lipstick-faced Demon, The Man with Fire on His Face and the Red-faced Man, is an entity of pure evil. He seeks passing from the Further into our world, and to do so he attempts to possess a human body. This ghoulish monster has a red and black face, white eyes with tiny black dots for pupils and a mouth of viciously sharp teeth. While he only appears in flashes in the real world (including one of the most heart-stopping scares in horror when he pops up in broad daylight without warning), a trip to the Further in the later acts of the original movie gives us a better look at the world the demon calls home.

Sitting busily in his lair, sharpening his lengthy claws while listening to a jaunty tune by Tiny Tim, this ghastly insidious monster treads the line between fascinating and downright nightmare fuel. But, like all of the best movie creatures, he does his job. There are plenty of other ghostly spirits who inhabit the world of the *Insidious* series, but the red demon's constantly lurking presence brings a dread like no other. Whether he is chasing our protagonists through the Further, or lurking ominously in the corner of a bedroom, this demon is sure to stay on your mind long after the film ends.

The Man with Fire on His Face – © Sony Pictures Releasing

IF IT'S IN A WORD, OR IT'S IN A LOOK...

The Babadook

Created by : Jennifer Kent
Appearances : *The Babadook* (2014)

The Babadook (2014) is a nerve-shredding psychological and supernatural horror. Sure to affect viewers in different ways, this ghost story focuses on the strained relationship between a mother and her son. Amelia's son Samuel begins to exhibit strange behaviour, from anti-social to obsessive to paranoid. Speaking of an entity called The Babadook, Samuel becomes dreamlike and hostile, forcing Amelia to seek psychological help for the six year-old boy.

As the drama heightens, Amelia soon becomes victim to the Babadook's visits as she begins to question both her sanity and her capability to relate to her son, who she now realises was telling the truth. The Babadook is a classic spook, creeping into dark corners, slowly opening bedroom doors to lurk about the bed and haunting the small family with his eccentric and terrifying form.

The Babadook as he appears in Samuel's book –
© Entertainment One

The Babadook – © *Entertainment One*

The ghost is a dark, top-hat wearing spectre with a white face and cold, piercing eyes. With no set movement, it is seen to float about, appear at will and haunt wherever it pleases, as well as influence the mood of Amelia and Samuel, causing harsh, expletive-filled arguments and shame.

The Babadook does easily what can be so tough for ghost and monster movies to achieve. It manages to create a new, excellent cinematic spirit that is memorable and truly scary, while also grounding the terror in a human story of grief, regret and sadness. The acting is superb and sells the terror just as much as the human drama.

This horrifying ghoul stands in for something we have all felt in our lives, and gives a tangible form to the grief and uncertainty that can haunt our daily lives. You can't get rid of the Babadook...

Ghosts can be thought of as corporeal beings or entities made of light. They can be invisible, making their presence known with the movement of objects or a bump in the night. But in some films, these spirits go beyond simply spooking here and there, and transform into something else entirely. They are grief, despair, fear and, most commonly of all, they are absolutely terrifying!

CHAPTER 5

BEST OF B-MOVIES

That site definitely wasn't the most sanitary you've worked on. Stripping off your clothes that are caked in concrete and dust, all you need is a shower to freshen up and a nap to kill some time and feel brand new. Your arm is still itchy where that weird stuff from the crumbling wall dripped, but you know you have some topical cream in the medicine cabinet. You apply it in front of the mirror and smile; the cooling relief takes away some of the itch and you leave it sit for a few minutes before you climb into a soothing shower. Lathering some shower gel you get to scrubbing the worries of the day away.

Your aching muscles feel the touch of the warm water and you continue to smile, knowing the sweet embrace of your cosy bed awaits. But then, you realise you've dropped a huge glob of shampoo to the shower floor. Dammit! You squat to try to scoop it up... but the shower gel was blue. This is red. Glancing to the itchy spot you see nothing but white. Your bone. The sludge flowing thick down the shower drain is you: your skin, your muscles, your blood. What did that toxic gloop do??? You try to scream but your lips have melted into a searingly painful jelly, that drips over your chest and lands by your feet with a wet slap. You groan as your eyes begin to burn.

Rocky Horror – © 20th Century Fox

You try to rub them but everything turns black as they too turn to goo in your melting fingers. Down the drain your form goes, joining the waste and sewage of the city as your bones remain on the shower floor. You manage one last horrifying scream as your sludgy, mutant form follows the pipes into the cavernous labyrinth below...

Rocky Horror

Common Strengths   : Charm, seduction, super strength
Common Weaknesses : Low intelligence, infatuation, emotional

Sometimes, the best thing about movie monsters is their ability to make us laugh. Whether it's through campy musical adventures or over-the-top gorefests that are so ludicrous in their execution you can't help but laugh, B-movies have brought the schlock we so badly crave for decades. With ingenious designs stemming from low budgets or simply due to the eccentricities of the creators, B-movie creatures have as much a place in monster history as demons, wolves and zombies.

TIME IS FLEETING...

Rocky Horror

Created by   : Richard O'Brien
Appearances : *The Rocky Horror Show* (1973 – stage show), *The Rocky Horror Picture Show* (1975), *The Rocky Horror Picture Show: Let's Do the Time Warp Again* (2016)

The 1975 whimsical, musical rollercoaster, *The Rocky Horror Picture Show*, brought to screen from the stage show by the eccentric Richard O'Brien, brings a colourful cast of bizarre characters to audiences.

Dr. Frank-N-Furter (Tim Curry) – © 20th Century Fox

Included in this book for its gothic sensibilities and its monstrous creation, Rocky, the film is the very definition of a cult classic. Modern screenings still occur, to massive fanfare, with audience members encouraged to dress up as their favourite characters.

Janet and Brad are in for the time of their lives when their car breaks down outside a mysterious castle during a storm. Looking for refuge, they stumble upon the dream-like world of Dr. Frank-N-Furter; a "sweet transvestite, from transsexual, Transylvania". In actuality, he is an alien from the planet Transsexual in the galaxy of Transylvania, and a brilliant but crazed scientist who is devoid of empathy and obsessed with creating the perfect man. With his loyal servants, Riff Raff and Magenta, he does so, and he shows his creation, Rocky, to the patrons of the annual Transylvanian convention, which he is hosting in his castle.

Sexually charged and manipulative, the doctor has no qualms in messing around with his new guests, trying to seduce both of them and using his perfect man to work his charms on them too. The flamboyance of the catchy musical numbers cleverly frame the impure intentions of Frank-N-Furter.

From butchering a poor delivery boy and serving him as food, to turning his guests into living statues, the devious doctor is addicted to his debauchery.

Rocky, on the other hand, is a mostly innocent soul. A monster purely owing to his creation, the muscular blond alpha is vain and infatuated with his creator and lover, Dr. Frank-N-Furter. In similar circumstances to Dr. Frankenstein and his monster, Frank-N-Furter and Rocky are alien and creature, although the relationship they share couldn't be more different.

Rocky is almost as promiscuous as the man who designed him, but his childlike innocence shows when danger rears its head. In the final act of the movie, which sees some of Frank-N-Furter's servants begin to question their master's intentions, Rocky is seen as conflicted and defensive of his creator, giving the hunk some empathy that betrays his monstrous origins.

The cast have been played by a vast array of actors throughout the many stage and film adaptations of the show. The ever-fantastic Tim Curry gives a career-highlight performance in the 1975 movie as Frank-N-Furter, imbuing the doctor with the kind of eccentricities that only he can conjure. Rocky and Dr. Frank-N-Furter were played by Staz Nair and Laverne Cox respectively in the 2016 TV-movie remake, *The Rocky Horror Picture Show: Let's Do the Time Warp Again*.

Frank-N-Furter (Tim Curry), Rocky (Peter Hinwood) and Janet (Susan Sarandon) – © 20th Century Fox

STUFF THAT!...

The Stuff

Created by : Larry Cohen
Appearances : *The Stuff* (1985)

"Kids and grown ups hate it so, the crazy alien marshmallow!"

When an odd, spongy white substance is found by railway construction workers, one taste of the creamy goo rockets it on a path to nationwide popularity. Sold to the public as 'The Stuff', the sweet treat is an addictive and popular dessert-style snack, overtaking the more traditional sugary goodies with ease.

In the midst of this new craze, its diversity betrays a more insidious side effect. When further tests are completed on the nature of the white substance, it's found to be a living organism. Sadly, all too late is the discovery that the stuff is parasitic, altering the host's biology and gradually deteriorating their mental capacity to an odd, zombie-like state.

Tragically (and far too often, comically) the stuff then hollows out the host and spews itself from their orifices, killing them. This showcases some entertaining,

The Stuff – © New World Pictures

THE ULTIMATE BOOK OF MOVIE MONSTERS

practical horror effects, with the white goo dramatically pouring from their bodies in a fairly horrific and definitive way; there's no way back once the stuff has gotten hold of you.

The Stuff (1985)is a unique monster movie, one that relies on the tragic consequences of something that ends up being too good to be true. Because of its nature, it's hard to feel anger at its actions, but more of a pity is felt for those unfortunate enough to consume the living gloop. Proving the addictive nature of the substance, the craze of seeking it out and eating as much as possible continues even after the fatal effects are revealed.

In many ways, *The Stuff* feels like a homage to the alien creature features of the past, but it's a unique take that blends '80s horror sensibilities with themes of consumerism and addiction, making for a genuinely entertaining flick with a stand-out, if non-descript, monster at its core.

FEED ME!...

Audrey II

Created by : Charles B. Griffith
Appearances : *The Little Shop of Horrors* (1960 – as Audrey Jr.), *Little Shop of Horrors* (1982 – musical show), *Little Shop of Horrors* (1986)

The darkly-comic musical, *Little Shop of Horrors* (1986) marries horror and earworm musical numbers in a completely unique way. Directed by Frank Oz and starring Rick Moranis, among other comedy legends, the movie is based on the 1960s film *The Little Shop of Horrors*. Seymour Krelborn finds himself wrapped up in the fanfare surrounding a unique plant he has named 'Audrey II', after his romantic interest, Audrey. While Audrey II is a rare plant initially intended to draw in more customers to the flower shop in which Seymour works, it begins to wither away despite attempts to nourish it.

Seymour fatefully feeds the plant some of his own blood after a cut, and makes a horrifying discovery. The plant thrives on human blood, and it soon begins to manipulate and demand more from Seymour in order to gather its strength, promising him fame and fortune if he does so. Against a backdrop of musical genius, this twisted flick melds genres deftly, delivering comedic moments amidst twisted and horrific scenarios. With a brilliant cast and stunning puppetry, the tragic tale of meek Seymour and his downward spiral is a classic slice of '80s nostalgia, and one of the more unique musical movies to come from Hollywood.

Audrey II is as physically entrancing as it is emotionally domineering. The massive crew needed to operate the Audrey II puppet do stunning work in making the malevolent creature expressive and intimidating. Sporting a large, gaping maw, not too dissimilar to a Venus fly trap, the plant makes short work of unfortunate victims, and plays a psychological game that preys on vulnerable folk like Seymour, coercing him into wicked and deadly deeds. While the songs keep the tone light for a chunk of the runtime, they are usually at odds with the dark goings-on which are orchestrated by the bloodthirsty plant.

Audrey II and Seymour (Rick Moranis) – © Warner Bros. Pictures

THE ULTIMATE BOOK OF MOVIE MONSTERS

For its insidious nature, faux-niceties, physical brutality and high-grade singing chops, Audrey II is a memorable, quotable and original movie monster that terrifies and delights in equal measure!

THIIIIIIIINK PINK!...

The Blob

Created by : Kay Linaker, Theodore Simonson, Irvin Yeaworth
Appearances : *The Blob* (1958), *Beware! The Blob* (1972), *The Blob* (1988)

The Blob, brought to life in the 1958 original and a hyper-violent 1988 remake, is a malevolent mass of pinkish goo, with impossible strength and a mindless mission to kill and absorb all living things it comes across.

The Blob (1988) – © TriStar Pictures

The Blob consumes a victim –
© TriStar Pictures

The remake of *The Blob* features the oozing creature as it goes on a violent rampage. Using its formless body to squeeze into small spaces, it leaves victims nowhere to run. The thinnest gap at the bottom of a locked door, the most constricting sewage pipe... the Blob will find a way to get you. It might use one of its many spontaneously erupting appendages to grasp you with an iron grip, sealing your fate as you are dragged into its humongous form and melted alive to join its ever-growing mutant body.

The gore on show in *The Blob* is stellar. Before the days of abundant CGI and blink-and-you'll-miss-'em practical effects, the '80s brought the ick factor with over-the-top, violent deaths, and *The Blob* is a perfect example of that commitment to gross-out, yet undeniably impressive, kills.

Seeing a full-grown man being pulled down a regular sink drain is an event not soon forgotten, and the tortured, melted visage of a recently engulfed victim is as disgusting as it is hilarious. While it is a classic monster movie, *The Blob* is teeming with gross moments that are so exaggerated they're sure to provide either nervous chuckles or all-out laughter.

As it consumes, it continues to grow in power, to the point that the whole town is at the mercy of the non-negotiable entity. Those who remain are left in desperation to find a way to stop something that has immense strength, yet can become diverse and permeable at will. *The Blob* might sound silly as a movie monster on paper, but in practice it's a truly scary antagonist, something far less concrete and relatively straightforward as a vampire, zombie or kaiju!

THE ULTIMATE BOOK OF MOVIE MONSTERS

REX GON' GIVE IT TO YA...

Rawhead Rex

Created by : Clive Barker

Appearances : *Books of Blood, Volume 3* (1984 – short story anthology), *Rawhead Rex* (1986)

The terror comes thick, fast and nine feet tall in an idyllic village in the Irish countryside. The demonic Rawhead Rex has risen from the grave, and he is out for blood. Given a bizarre religious backstory, this hulking abomination

Rawhead Rex – @ Empire Pictures

goes on an unstoppable rampage, leaving absolute bloody carnage in his wake. With his glowing red eyes, a jutting maw of deadly teeth and a hairy, ape-like body, Rex is a true terror, even if his appearance is borderline comical.

Those looking for serious, slow-burn horror need not apply, as master of terror, Clive Barker, brings one of his more off-the-wall and tonally unique monsters to the screen. Barker penned the script, but would later lament the appearance of the demon, disappointed that it did not match the description given in his short story (in which he describes Rawhead Rex as a nine-foot phallus).

Full to the brim with bizarre imagery (such as a baptism involving urine) and gory kills, *Rawhead Rex* (1986) is certainly an acquired taste, and its target audience might not seem obvious. If you like over-the-top acting, an admittedly effective monster for the most part (especially when he shows up outside a family's parked car in broad daylight for a snack) and awful Irish accents galore, you'll have a good time with it. It's definitely not pretending to be something it's not, so if you can accept the ludicrous monster and premise, *Rawhead Rex* should give you decent creature carnage entertainment.

WAKE AND BAKE... AND DIE!...

Evil Bong

Created by	: Charlie Band and August White
Appearances	: *Evil Bong* (2006), *Evil Bong 2: King Bong* (2009), *Evil Bong 3D: The Wrath of Bong* (2011), *Gingerdead Man vs. Evil Bong* (2013), *Evil Bong 420* (2015), *Evil Bong High-5!* (2016), *Evil Bong 666* (2017), *Evil Bong 777* (2018)

Movie legend Tommy Chong went toe-to-pipe with the Evil Bong, later christened Eebee, in the first movie of the long-running stoner horror series. Following the misadventures of various groups of herb enthusiasts, *Evil Bong* is movie monster with no real comparison.

Evil Bong – © *Full Moon Features*

She is exactly what the title describes: an evil, sentient bong with facial features and a sassy attitude. Initially, Eebee seems like a blessing, as one toke from her mystical form transports users to the Bong World, a place where debauchery and constant party is the order of the day. But, as many unfortunates discover throughout the cult series, Bong World is an evil place, and things that once seemed too good to be true turn out to be... just that.

The malevolent dimension sets rabid, murderous strippers on the antagonists, as well as finding our unlucky heroes in the presence of King Bong, a jungle-dwelling, colossal bong who has a long-standing rivalry with Eebee. Not content with being confined to one apartment, Eebee's adventures of terror have spread to Las Vegas, space, and have even seen her come to blows with the B-movie slasher, the Gingerdead Man.

In *Gingerdead Man vs. Evil Bong*, the two low-budget monsters trade quips and are vying for the schlock-horror crown, with the usual group of unwitting fodder caught in the middle. Eebee's unique power and inter-dimensional influence make her a worthy foe for the Gingerdead Man, and the irony of these two 'baked' icons facing off is not lost on the filmmakers, who throw everything but the kitchen sink into the climactic showdown.

King Bong – © *Full Moon Features*

Eebee's popularity shows no signs of slowing down, and the demon pipe will surely terrorise the small screen with more 'high' quality scares in the years to come.

B-movies often bring the gore to the forefront, allowing for spectacularly 'out-there' storylines and creatures that deftly mix hilarity, implausibility and frights in equal measure. Often used to parody modern culture or cinematic trends (such as in the 1978 satirical monster movie *Attack of the Killer Tomatoes*), they are usually great movie monsters for enjoying with friends or in an ironic way, ensuring plenty of laughter. Conversely, they can be genuine masterpieces of cinema, the films that are not afraid to push boundaries and buck industry trends with their eccentricities, and the creature-filled landscape of film is all the better for them.

CHAPTER 6

DEATH FROM THE DEPTHS

You always feel free on the open water. There's nothing quite like the sea air to take away the blues and clear your mind. The water is calm, save for the gentle sloshing of tiny waves as your small, wooden kayak drifts around the scenic bay. Crystal blue waters give way to more muddy ones, but you're so relaxed right now, you're content to just let the world drift by. Your boat is suddenly shifted violently. You check the waters around but the surrounding area is calm, no sign of wind or disturbances. As you lean to peer into the murky waters, a second flurry of thumps cracks the side of the small boat and spins you, capsizing your vessel and leaving you submerged in the deep. As you struggle from under the overturned boat, something brushes by your leg rapidly. You look

around as your life vest hugs your chin and the sun beats down on the rippling water. Nothing... You make to turn the kayak and investigate the damage. But before you can, you find yourself pulled beneath the surface once again, this time, with force. The water feels warmer the further you plummet, but it's not the water... it's blood. Your blood. You pull your leg free from a pincer grip, but all that does is pull the flesh away more easily. Flailing in futility you somehow manage to breach the surface, and you spin wildly

Jaws – © Universal Pictures

to search for your boat, for safety. You scramble towards refuge, but it's too late. The other leg is jerked downward, you hear the crack, you feel the blood. Your legs are in a blender, the warmth of your own lifeforce surrounding you. And with that, your body is taken to the depths; the depths of the ocean, the depths of pain...

Jaws

Common Strengths   : Size, speed, razor-sharp teeth, stealth
Common Weaknesses : Harpoons, explosions

From the depths of the ocean have come some of the worst, dread-soaked terrors in all of cinema. Ranging from plausible beasties to otherworldly abominations, the big blue is clearly hiding some of the most terrifying monsters of all, and when we breach the briny deep, *we're* the intruders.

YOU'RE GONNA NEED A BIGGER BOAT...

Jaws

Created by   : Peter Benchley
Appearnces : *Jaws* (1974 – novel), *Jaws* (1975), Various different Great White Sharks
                    appear in *Jaws 2* (1978), *Jaws 3-D* (1983) and *Jaws: The Revenge* (1987)

When it comes to perils that strike from the endless blue, few on-screen beasts live in the public zeitgeist as heavily as the mighty Jaws. This terrifying Great White shark is a vicious and deadly predator, and it provides tragedy after tragedy for the unfortunate residents of Amity Island. Police Chief Martin

Sheriff Brody (Roy Scheider) vs. Jaws – © Universal Pictures

Brody is the first to fully comprehend the terror that lurks around the beaches of Amity, and it isn't long before his suspicions prove gravely correct.

Jaws is known for its memorable opening scene, along with a minimalistic main theme from John Williams that is recognisable worldwide, even by people who have never seen the film. The animatronics on show are incredible and still hold up well today, and the gargantuan Great White himself is as imposing a presence off-screen as he is on. The hysteria as victims try to escape the predator creates countless moments of panic and fear, as one of humanity's worst nightmares is brought to life on film – the fear of being pulled beneath the depths by an unseen force of nature. It's definitely best not to watch this movie before a beach trip.

Jaws made enough of an impact to warrant the creature getting three follow-ups, although none of these matched the perfect mix of terror and adventure that Steven Spielberg's original did. Turning Peter Benchley's novel into a pulse-pounding Hollywood tentpole was no easy task, but Spielberg's deft hand helped to craft a timeless classic. *Jaws'* legacy lives on through the film series, parodies and the Universal Studios theme park attraction, where passengers are treated to an immersive boat ride, complete with a devastating attack by the creature itself and a daring and heroic boat captain. If you let *Jaws* and the all too relatable fear associated with him get under your skin, it will NEVER be safe to go back in the water...

FEEDING FRENZY...

Piranha

Created by : John Sayles

Appearances : *Piranha* (1978), *Piranha II: The Spawning* (1982), *Piranha* (1995), *Piranha 3D* (2010), *Piranha 3DD* (2012)

Following the cinematic influence of the Great White, a number of pretenders and parodies made their presence known. In 1978, the prolific creature master Joe Dante brought the campy classic *Piranha* to the silver screen. It 'spawned' a series of sequels and remakes all using more or less the same premise of swarms of the deadly, razor-toothed fish making short work of unsuspecting civilians.

The genetically altered demon fish take no prisoners as they attack and guzzle the hapless people of Lost River, bypassing attempts to poison them and

Piranha – © United Artists

prevent their entrance into the oceans of the world. They are the remnant of a long-forgotten experiment in biological warfare designed to send schools of the deadly fish to war and put an end to the Viet Cong.

The disastrous results live on in the form of the pack-hunting schools of mutated piranha who see no difference in adult or child on their quest to kill. If you dip so much as a toe in the water you may well disappear beneath a burst of your own blood and viscera. In a last-ditch attempt to stop the chaotic fish, river guide Grogan plans to release waste into the water and kill the frenzied animals once and for all. The final act is a desperate race against time and teeth, and the ferocity of the piranha is shown in all its bloody glory.

An antidote to the drama of the *Jaws* series, *Piranha* has gone on to birth its own school of cult fans, and they remain in the underwater creature feature zeitgeist to this day.

MY ANACONDA DON'T WANT NONE...

Anacondas

Created by : Hans Bauer, Luis Llosa, Jack Epps Jr., Jim Cash

Appearances : *Anaconda* (1997), *Anacondas: The Hunt for the Blood Orchid* (2004), *Anaconda 3: Offspring* (2008), *Anacondas: Trail of Blood* (2009), *Lake Placid vs. Anaconda* (2015)

Anaconda (1997) features an ensemble cast that includes Jon Voight, Jennifer Lopez, Ice Cube and Owen Wilson. They face off against the titular 40-foot snake in the Amazon jungle, and the deadly beast thins their numbers with alarming ease.

Part adventure, part creature feature, the anaconda of the title is a gargantuan beast, thick with muscle and bearing deadly white fangs and an

Anaconda – © Sony Pictures Releasing

unsavoury habit which sees it partially digest its prey before regurgitating it for re-consumption.

The murky waters hide the beast well, leaving the documentary crew in a constant state of vulnerability. With its crushing strength, near-silent traversal and ability to gobble anyone who's off their guard in a matter of seconds, the anaconda is a formidable beast. Easily moving about on land and water, it's versatile in its execution and with a combination of computer-generated effects and animatronics it comes to life in variety of ways, some more convincing than others.

The 1997 original, *Anaconda*, is a classic '90s adventure, complete with brutal kills and larger-than-life characters. It was followed by *Anacondas: The Hunt for the Blood Orchid* (2004), the *Aliens* equivalent to the original, with a whole host of the giant snakes hunting a new cast of characters. The beasts returned again for third and fourth installments, which went even bigger on the cheese factor thanks to veteran actor David Hasselhoff. The crushing cretins also faced off against the massive crocodiles of the *Lake Placid* series, in *Lake Placid vs. Anaconda* (2015).

WE'RE GONNA NEED A BIGGER CHOPPER...

Sharknado Sharks

Created by : Thunder Levin and Anthony C. Ferrante

Appearances : *Sharknado* (2013), *Sharknado 2: The Second One* (2014), *Sharknado 3: Oh Hell No!* (2015), *Sharknado: The 4th Awakens* (2016), *Sharknado 5: Global Swarming* (2017), *The Last Sharknado: It's About Time* (2018)

Sharknado burst onto the scene in 2013, produced by legendary B-movie and parody production company, The Asylum. By now, most of the movie-going world knows the score. A tornado forms and begins to ensnare and then blast out sharks, making them rain down upon Los Angeles where they cause murder and mayhem for those unfortunate enough to get in their way.

Currently six films deep – although *The Last Sharknado* at least hints at a definitive end for the series – the movies are built to give the people what they want; cheesy dialogue, improbable storylines and gory kills executed with low-budget special effects, to hilarious results.

Sharknado 2: The Second One – © *The Asylum*

Featuring innumerable cameos from famous faces, from All Elite Wrestling and former WWE and WCW wrestling superstar Chris Jericho to twin Irish pop sensations Jedward, the *Sharknado* series needs to be appreciated for its willingness to commit to its premise and deliver laughs and kills a minute. It simultaneously sheds a light on how ludicrous the premises of many creature features are, and having gotten its own lore out of the way early on, the filmmakers let the sharks do the talking... and brutal murdering.

A movie loosely tied to the *Sharknado* movies by the inclusion of a cameo of the main character, Fin Shepard (yes, really), is *Lavalantula* (2015), which, as you may have guessed, is about fire-spitting spiders. It was popular enough to spawn a sequel, *2 Lava 2 Lantula*, in 2016. If *Sharknado* isn't enough to get your underwater terror fix, The Asylum also produced four *Mega Shark* movies (*Mega Shark vs. Giant Octopus, Mega Shark vs. Crocosaurus, Mega Shark vs. Mecha Shark* and *Mega Shark vs. Kolossus*, 2009–2015), with a fifth, *Mega Shark vs. Moby Dick*, in early production.

Stick any of these nonsense movies on at a gathering and you're guaranteed a good time. You can laugh with it, you can laugh at it and you can subject yourself to the highest form of avant-garde art known to man. Or something like that. Enough said. Fin.

NATIONAL LAGOON'S TERRIFYING VACATION...

The Creature from the Black Lagoon

Created by : William Alland
Appearances : *Creature from the Black Lagoon* (1954), *Revenge of the Creature* (1955), *The Creature Walks Among Us* (1956)

One of the most unique and animalistic monsters from the Universal era is *Creature from the Black Lagoon* (1954). This aquatic-humanoid monstrosity

Creature from the Black Lagoon – © *Universal Pictures*

becomes the obsession of scientists who believe it to be the missing link between humans and what once dwelled underwater.

With a distinctly fish-like appearance, including a large, guppy-like mouth and gills, the creature is a stealthy, stalking menace. It picks off the team with ease, as it moves swiftly through the weeds and murky water of the Black Lagoon. While mostly a silent onlooker, the beast is shown to concoct plans for trapping and eliminating its new enemies. Becoming infatuated with a female member, Kay, the beast follows her every move, including an atmospheric scene where it swims beneath her as she moves about the deep waters. The score accentuates the slow-building dread as it moves nearer, before retreating into the reeds and biding its time.

Atmospheric and uniquely stylish, *Creature from the Black Lagoon* is rightly revered and remembered as one of Universal's most unnerving monsters. Whereas the Great White in *Jaws* is somewhat rooted in plausibility and is purely animalistic, this legendary predator is disturbingly mixed in its habits, formulating plans but, more often than not, letting its hunting instincts get the better of it. It influenced countless movies to come, both serious in their tone and humorous in their execution (the creature feature horror, *Humanoids from the Deep* from 1980 is a great example of this).

One can only hope for a modern reimagining of this brilliant and influential film.

THE GIRL FROM IPANEMA...

The Octalus

Created by : Stephen Sommers
Appearances : *Deep Rising* (1998)

The action-packed, seafaring adventure, *Deep Rising* (1998) is a full-throttle creature feature full of one-liners, memorable and larger-than-life characters and ferocious, monstrous threats. It's an undeniably good time, following the exploits of Finnegan (Treat Williams) as he is drawn into an organised robbery of a luxury cruise liner. The mercenaries' monetary quest is the least of everyone's problems, as the gang are soon attacked by beings altogether evil, risen from the depths of the ocean and seeking murderous mayhem.

The creatures of *Deep Rising* are tooth-filled tentacles; limber monsters that stalk the many corridors and passages of the *Argonautica*, bringing chaos and death upon those unfortunate enough to cross their paths. The chemistry of the cast ensures the hammy dialogue and over-the-top kills are as entertaining as possible, and despite the mixed tone, the movie shows a lot of heart in its confidence, revelling in its influences from the great sci-fi horrors of the past. It's a cult film with a mostly original setting. Like *From Dusk Till Dawn*, it takes a classic espionage template, brings it to the open water and throws a bucketful of slaughter into the mix.

The unpredictability makes it a perfect late-night watch with friends, and the revelation of the creature's origins is inspired, giving an eerie and catastrophic context to the beings' presence. If you like sarcastic comedy and genuinely exciting adventure in your horror, *Deep Rising* is a sure-fire hit.

What lurks beneath the water of our planet is more unknown than much of our world, or even our galaxy. Through film, directors, producers and writers have penned and created fear from this uncertainty, making both existing creatures terrifying on-screen forces and conjuring new, deathly threats with which to scare the wits out of film fans. The effective, floundering panic continues to forge its own unique niche in cinema, from the Lovecraftian creature feature *Underwater* (2020) to the shark-infested water of the *47 Metres Down* series. These vicious creatures keep audiences entertained by plunging into the very depths of terror...

A tentacle creature from Deep Rising *– © Buena Vista Pictures*

CHAPTER 7

TERROR FROM ABOVE

The corn fields are the perfect place for you and your friends to have some beers and a smoke. You've never seen anyone else out here, and the old man that lives on the farm never comes out of his house after 8pm. And that dog of his is so old it couldn't catch a half-dead rabbit. You feel yourself getting tipsy as the laughter rings around you. The stars are bright tonight, and you can't help but gaze upwards and dream into the night. The drink is good, the company is good... what more could you want? You keep your head tilted back and close your eyes as you listen to the warm, gentle breeze rustle the field and the boisterous laughter of your best buddies ring out. But

Xenomorph – © 20th Century Fox

those laughs turn to gasps, and you shake yourself from your momentary haze. What the hell? The cornfields are aglow, beginning to burn, and a green hue has fallen across the countryside.

"What the hell is THAT?" you hear one of your friends call out, but before anyone can answer, a mammoth of metal has collided with the earth, sending a sonic boom about the farm that makes you all grasp your ears in pain. A hiss follows, and an unearthly noise. Like a chant in some ancient Latin, it begins to get louder through the ringing in your ears. Humanoid shapes are approaching your group, but these are no humans. Over ten feet tall, with dark-grey, hulking bodies, they storm forwards with intent. You count six in your immediate vicinity, but you see more drop from the massive craft behind. The closest one roars something incomprehensible, before raising a weapon, and vaporising your closest friend, who didn't even get a chance to scream. You try to scream for him, but a muscular, three-fingered hand clasps itself around your throat. The being before you stares at you with a thick, furrowed brow. They are not of this world. And soon, neither are you. It cracks your throat and places the weapon into your stomach. A blast of green... and you are no more...

Xenomorph

Common Strengths	: Stealth, super senses, acidic blood, extra mouth, spiked tail, crushing grip
Common Weaknesses	: Firearms, fire, space jettison, Ellen Ripley, the *Predator* species

Every now and then, an extra-terrestrial presence goes past the point of mere science fiction and into the realms of full-blown horror. While usually the subject of misunderstanding and an overarching mystery, on many occasions an otherworldly invasion can bring with it terrifying creatures that seek only to kill and destroy. The following are some movie aliens that forego the romanticism of visitors from another world and delve straight into absolute destruction.

THE PERFECT ORGANISM...

Xenomorph (*Alien*)

Created by : Dan O'Bannon, Ridley Scott, H.R. Giger

Appearances : *Alien* (1979), *Aliens* (1986), *Alien 3* (1992), *Alien Resurrection* (1997), *Alien vs. Predator* (2004), *Aliens vs. Predator: Requiem* (2007), *Prometheus* (2012 – in engineer-born form, the Deacon), *Alien: Covenant* (2017 – both Neomorph and Xenomorph forms), Countless novels, comic books and video games

Terrorising the screen for over forty years, the creature known as the xenomorph or more commonly referred to outside the films as the alien, is arguably the most pure cinematic monster that has ever existed. The series, which began with the legendary original *Alien* in 1979, has continued to draw in both science-fiction and horror lovers for decades. The eponymous creature is a lethal hunter, with a slick, elongated head and a set of oozing teeth that hides a second, pulsing maw that it can propel forward to burst into the flesh of its extremely unlucky victims. Designed by the legendary artist H.R. Giger - originating from his painting, Necronom IV - the xenomorph has been mostly resigned to the shadows, hunting Ellen Ripley and the crew of the *Nostromo* in the tension-filled first installment, which instantly propelled it into the annals of horror movie history.

Though the initial movie and the third film, *Alien 3* (1992), only featured one of the creatures, the rest of the series, including the crossovers with the '80s classic creature, *Predator*, featured masses of the hunters. While they have been killed with the persistent use of firearms, blunt force or ejection into space, they are formidable threats to humans, silently hunting from above, or impregnating hosts using 'facehuggers'. These spider-like creatures, with their terrifying speed and vice-like strength, clasp themselves to the faces of their prey, and, using an extending fleshy tube, lay eggs through the oesophagus and into the victim's chest cavity. In some of the most horrific scenes in the franchise (which has expanded since the '70s to include novels, comics, video

A xenomorph in Aliens – © 20ᵗʰ Century Fox

games and a TV series), the newborn xenomorphs burst from the chests of the unfortunates, instantly killing them and bringing a newly-formed horror into the world.

The prequel series, which began with 2012's *Prometheus* and continued in 2017's *Alien: Covenant*, offered in-depth origins for the species fans had been

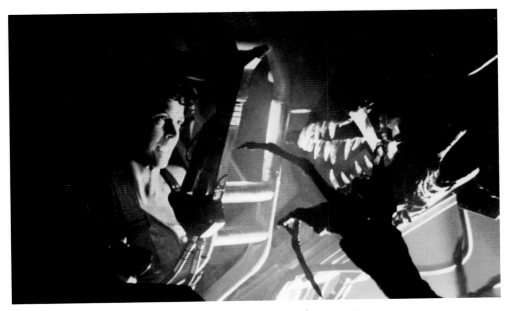

Ellen Ripley (Sigourney Weaver) and an Alien Queen – © 20ᵗʰ Century Fox

enamoured with for the preceding decades. Offering some interesting answers to mysteries seen in Ridley Scott's original vision, his prequels meshed the space opera genre with pure terror, offering grisly scenes of body-horror that mix perfectly with the existential crises the characters face as they explore the origins of life on Earth. The physically intimidating Engineers - tall, brutish, unfeeling humanoids - lead the antagonists on an interstellar journey that twists and turns and slowly leads to the birth of the murderous star beast that populated the original four movies.

Hiding in the dark of various crafts and stations, the xenomorph can traverse entire ships with ease, swiftly moving about ventilation tunnels and masterfully blending its body into the various, pipe-filled corridors. As the series progressed, it was revealed that the physiology of the xenomorph would depend on the host body it burst from. This makes the journey to finding the original xeno from the first installment one that's full of twists and shocks, remaining completely unpredictable throughout *Prometheus* and *Alien: Covenant*. The android, David (Michael Fassbender) who is a crew member of the *Prometheus* ship and develops a fascination with the Engineers and their ability to provide life to worlds and terrain, is instrumental in the genesis of the creatures as we know them in the original series of films.

The unfortunate Ellen Ripley is forced to watch her companions fall victim to the xenomorph threat repeatedly, as her life is dominated by the nightmare creatures. This is made worse by the fact that she must continually prove her sanity and convince new groups of the existence of the aliens and their

An engineer in Prometheus – © 20th *Century Fox*

devastating hostility. Time after time, the people surrounding Ripley are impregnated by facehuggers, burst through by the jutting teeth of the beasts or burned by the creature's acidic blood, a defence mechanism that catches plenty of crews off guard. Even with a squad of colonial marines on the case, the xenomorphs are too powerful to be stopped and easily pick off the majority of the crew through their speed and deadliness.

Serving to populate the ships and facilities of the various films, comics and novels is usually an alien Queen. This massive creature can lay a multitude of eggs, from which hatch the dreaded facehuggers. These, in turn, find their hosts and begin the birthing process. Thanks to their streamlined evolution, the baby xenomorphs reach full growth in a fraction of the time that most other creatures do. This allows them to rapidly populate and dominate any region they can get a hold of. The Queen herself is also a formidable enemy, with a mouth of vicious teeth that far outsizes those of its offspring. With a ridged and armoured crown-like head and huge, limber hands, the Queen is an absolute monstrosity, albeit one with an impeccable design for instilling fear and ensuring the preservation of its twisted species.

An alien Queen – © 20ᵗʰ Century Fox

The xenomorph threat shows no signs of slowing down, and with Disney's acquisition of the *Alien* parent company, 20th Century Fox, the terror will continue in a TV series utilising the mythology, as well as a Marvel comic book series. Remember: in space, no one can hear you scream...

POWER OF THE NIGHT...

Krites

Created by : Domonic Muir

Appearances : *Critters* (1986), *Critters 2: The Main Course* (1988), *Critters 3* (1991), *Critters 4* (1992), *Critters Attack!* (2019), *Critters: A New Binge* (2019 – TV series)

Vicious, calculating and stealthy, the krites are small statured extra-terrestrials that are so notorious they are tailed by intergalactic bounty hunters for their violent rampages. Resembling hedgehogs mixed with nightmares, they bear blood-red eyes, razor-sharp teeth and prickly spikes that they often use as projectiles to pierce and incapacitate their victims.

At only a foot or so tall, they are often mistaken for large rodents or other pests. This lulls the many victims throughout the five-movie *Critters* series into false senses of security, with bloody results. From terrorising a small town to battling with an emerging Leonardo DiCaprio (*Critters 3* was his film debut) in an apartment block and even taking the massacre to deep space for *Critters 4*, the krites are miniature forces to be reckoned with.

With speed (they can be seen to turn into balls and roll for effective traversal), ferocity and clever deception, hiding in the darkest spots and leaping to eviscerate unsuspecting victims, the krites continue their binge on Earth's unfortunate inhabitants.

Krites in Critters 2 – © *New Line Cinema*

YEAH, F@*K YOU TOO!...

The Thing

Created by : John W. Campbell, Rob Bottin, Stan Winston

Appearances : *Who Goes There?* (1938 – novella), *The Thing from Another World* (1951), *The Thing* (1982), *The Thing* (2002 – sequel video game), *The Thing* (2011 – prequel)

John Carpenter's *The Thing*, one of many adaptations of the novella *Who Goes There?*, is a 1982 sci-fi horror that features one of the most iconic extra-terrestrial threats in film history. Against the lonely backdrop of the Antarctic, a research crew comes across a frozen alien spacecraft. Unbeknownst to them, the being inside can assimilate and imitate living creatures, and they soon find themselves awash in paranoia and death as they attempt to deduce who among them has become host to the hostile life-form.

The Thing – © Universal Pictures

MacReady (Kurt Russell) investigates – © Universal Pictures

The practical and hyper-violent special effects bring the grisly transformations to life. Once the alien being has been found out in its host body, it tends to go on the offensive, transforming the unfortunate human (or canine!) into a deadly, mutated beast. Often found with extra limbs, several gaping maws and tendrils with which to grasp and annihilate the researchers and doctors that occupy the base, the thing from another planet sets about killing or assimilating the entire crew, although its long-term motives are never explored.

The movie is terrifying in its depiction of isolation and paranoia, and how crippling it can be to deal with constant suspicion and second-guessing of your actions in a life-or-death situation. Kurt Russell's R.J. MacReady is the main protagonist, and throughout the film he is forced to make crucial decisions on who can be trusted, a problem that comes to a head in the infamous blood test scene. In it, members of the team have their blood tested in Petri dishes through extreme heat as a way of discovering who has been assimilated. The tension is palpable, and the reveal is extremely unsettling and action-packed.

While not properly appreciated on release, *The Thing* has gone on to become revered as a masterpiece of sci-fi horror; from the brooding score by the late Ennio Morricone to the stellar special effects and not least of all due to the terror induced by one of film's most unrelenting and nefarious monsters. Carpenter's version of *The Thing* went on to spawn a video game sequel of the same name in 2002, and a 2011 prequel, also named simply *The Thing*, that leads directly into the events of the 1982 original. Both feature the same gruesome extra-terrestrial as it wreaks havoc in Antarctica.

IF IT BLEEDS, WE CAN KILL IT...

Predator

Created by : Jim Thomas, John Thomas

Appearances : *Predator (1987), Predator 2 (1990), Alien vs. Predator (2004), Aliens vs. Predator: Requiem (2007), Predators (2010), The Predator (2018), Prey (2022)*, Countless novels, comics and video games

Now intrinsically linked with the xenomorph, the creature that originated in 1987's *Predator* is both intriguing and lethal. A mostly humanoid creature, the Predator (or Yautja – pronounced Ya-Oot-Ja) dons metallic, tribal armour, including a mask which hides its fleshy, four-toothed mouth and beady eyes. With head dressing resembling dreadlocks, the ancient hunter is a master of stealth, carrying with it an array of useful gadgets and weaponry. Whether it's hunting soldiers in the rainforests of South America, tormenting the citizens of Los Angeles or turning a whole planet into a murderous playground, this species revels in the thrill of the hunt.

Certainly not as instinctual as the xenomorph, the Predator has been shown to be open to collaborations, even with humans under certain circumstances, and can have a high degree of honour, depending on the situation. Choosing their invasion points carefully, most Predators look for hunting grounds that

Predator – © 20th Century Fox

will challenge their skills and impress their kin, sometimes as a sort of rite of passage. In *Predator 2* (1990), the main monster chooses the busy city of Los Angeles, due in large part to the ongoing drug war that brings together two rival gangs and the LAPD, ensuring there is plenty of well-armed fodder for the hunt.

It can use a wrist-plate device to communicate with its ship, set off a self-destruct sequence and arm its explosive homing weapon. The creature utilises a cloaking device that makes its entire body and armour translucent, leaving it practically undetectable save for a slightly wobbling outline, almost imperceptible to the human eye. This allows the Predator to stalk its prey, learn patterns and gauge its weaponry. Likewise, the hunter can use heat-sensitive vision, which helps it to rapidly identify heat signatures that might equal human life. Not content with its expert spy technology, the Predator also commits to confusing the unfortunate fodder by utilising voice recordings. This deception causes sadness and fear, toying with emotions and spreading panic among the unfortunate victims of this apex alien.

A Super Predator in Predators *– © 20th Century Fox*

THE ULTIMATE BOOK OF MOVIE MONSTERS

COTTON CAN-DIE...

The Killer Klowns from Outer Space

Created by : Stephen, Charles and Edward Chiodo
Appearances : *Killer Klowns from Outer Space* (1988)

The most colourful of all the extra-terrestrial terrors to take to the screen are the *Killer Klowns from Outer Space* (1988). These mischievous monsters invade Earth with unsavoury purposes. More specifically, they invade with sweet purposes. Their bulbous bodies and demonic cackles are genuinely unsettling, but their partially comical appearances cause the residents of Crescent Cove to overlook their menace as some sort of elaborate prank. Their mistake.

The klowns go on a rampage; eating, murdering and wrapping their unfortunate victims in cotton candy cocoons to store in their mothership for later consumption. While many movie aliens have powers reasonably within

Killer Klowns from Outer Space – © *Trans World Entertainment*

Killer Klowns from Outer Space – © *Trans World Entertainment*

the realms of scientific explanation, the klowns are extra-terrestrial magicians, using shadow puppets to devour and kidnap bystanders for imprisonment on their mothership, blasting civilians with popcorn bazookas and bringing balloon animals to life to join in their rampage.

The ship itself resembles a massive circus tent, but the interior is a science-fiction maze of winding corridors and elevators, and it is here that the unfortunate humans are cocooned in candy floss. The final monstrosity the protagonists come across is a towering and terrifying puppet klown, seemingly a leader to the other known minions, who are constantly amassing klown larvae in the form of popcorn.

Killer Klowns from Outer Space is a riot. It's unashamedly cheesy, and leans into it, and the rubber suits and creature designs are fantastic – another example of tangible monsters leading to graceful aging of a production. That's not to say that only the practical effects are impressive. Watching a klown shrink a group of humans using a shadow puppet or a circus tent-shaped spaceship rise from Earth are so impressive you'd be forgiven if you thought the movie came out much later than 1988.

If you want to laugh and enjoy a silly horror movie with friends, this is the one to make it happen. Just make sure no one in your group has a fear of clowns!

THE ULTIMATE BOOK OF MOVIE MONSTERS

WHAT THE FLOCK?...

The Birds

Created by : Daphne du Maurier

Appearances : *The Birds* (1952 – as part of the short story collection *The Apple Tree*), *The Birds* (1963), *The Birds II: Land's End* (1994)

Alfred Hitchcock is mostly remembered for his psychological thrillers; stories about murder, deception and tales of paranoia and betrayal. But in 1963 he would direct one of his most unique and iconic films, *The Birds*. Based on the short story by Daphne du Maurier, it starred a sinister avian cast and would cement itself as an oft-referenced and lampooned cinematic classic.

The Birds – © *Universal Pictures*

In Bodega Bay, California, Melanie visits an old flame, Mitch, after buying two lovebirds from a San Francisco pet store. When she reaches Mitch's house in the bay, the local avian life begins to act strangely, attacking children and adults with zero provocation. When a neighbour ends up dead and eyeless, the gravity of the situation sets in, and the murderous birds only become more aggressive in their attempts to end human life.

Hitchcock succeeds on many levels with this creature feature. Making usually non-violent animals into feared monsters is an art in and of itself. There are many ways in which the premise could become ridiculous when portrayed on film, but through deft direction and fantastic effects, Alfred Hitchcock managed to pull off a thoroughly tense story filled with iconic imagery and a terrifyingly inescapable menace.

The sound design plays its role in the tension too, as seeing flocks of birds perched patiently in wait for their victims, in utter silence, is more unnerving than it has any right to be. With prolonged, wonderfully framed shots, Hitchcock creates a dense atmosphere, one that makes the audience realise just how terrifying this situation would be. A stark reminder that we are all at the mercy of nature, The Birds clicks on many levels as a white-knuckle thriller. Without motive, but nonetheless unnervingly threatening, the birds are unlike any other movie monsters, before or after.

IN FOR THE KILL...

The *Alien* and *Predator* franchises had crossed over in various stories in mediums beyond film. Comics and novels are usually more logistically sound for the kind of crazy mash-ups we rarely see in films, when two popular series are thrown into the mix together. When keen-eyed fans spotted a xenomorph skull on the Predators' trophy wall aboard their ship in the final act of *Predator 2*, the Hollywood rumour mill started to turn.

In 2004, director Paul W.S. Anderson (*Mortal Kombat*, the *Resident Evil* series) was the one to finally bring these two iconic monsters together for the dream match fans has been clamouring for. In *Alien vs. Predator*, the backdrop is

A Predator and a Xenomorph face off in AVP: Alien vs. Predator *– © 20ᵗʰ Century Fox*

Antarctica, and a team discovers a vast, underground pyramid which is giving off heat signatures. Upon entering, xenomorphs are released, and soon after, the Predators arrive to hunt what is revealed to be their choice prey.

The ensuing battle claims expendable human fodder as the Predator coming-of-age ritual plays out with violent consequences. Each species has their full powers on show, with the Predator utilising its full arsenal of weaponry and the xenomorphs showing stealth and cunning to take out their rivals.

A sequel followed in 2007, entitled *Aliens vs. Predator: Requiem*, and it saw the creatures once again do battle in a small town. This time around, a new creature is thrown into the mix in the form of the hybrid Predalien. Neither of the movies made much of an impact with fans, as the horror aspects of both franchises were jettisoned in favour of all-out action. If you dream of seeing these two alien creatures destroy each other in a plethora of nasty ways however, you might get a kick or two out of it.

From the sky and from the stars, the unknown terrors lurking above our heads have made for some of the finest outings in horror cinema. Offering legendary creatures like the xenomorph and the Predator, among riotously enjoyable goblins like the krites, these movie monsters will have you gazing at the stars and wondering if there really is intelligent life out there... and whether we even want to know about it...

The Predalien in Aliens vs. Predator: Requiem – @ 20th Century Fox

CHAPTER 8

CURSED CALAMITIES

As the door creaks open, you hear the bubbling of water, and the heat and smell hit you. What IS that? You hold your nose and grimace. The air inside is putrid and through the darkness you struggle to make anything out. There is a regular CLINK, CLINK sound as you slowly tiptoe across the rotted wood of the cabin floor. And, sure enough, something in the centre of the room is moving. Circular motions are all you can see - a thick, elongated implement twirling about as though it were being blown by the wind.

At once, it stops, and you stick a hand forward to feel the now stationery ladle that sits inside a massive, black cauldron. You frown as you gaze inside, and, just as you do, a beam of bright moonlight creeps through one of the only clear windows

in the entire grimy stead. The putrid stuff inside is a sickly olive-green colour, and the smell has only gotten worse the closer you moved. Suddenly, you hear a clatter of glass bottles collapse in the corner of the room. As you glance, you see a blurred shape whiz to the other side of the room, into shadow. The glint of the moon barely bounces from the thick fluid still bubbling before you.

Werewolf

You turn again... it's a full moon. The howl sounds as if it is coming from inside your head, and with no time to prepare, you hear the scrabbling at the door. The sound of claws, of growling, of sniffing and grunting. And then, as if bursting forth from behind a curtain, a crooked old hag zooms towards you, a rusty, short blade grasped tightly in her hand. You duck, and as you do, you realise she wasn't coming for you at all.

The door bursts down and a monstrous, wolf-like creature leaps towards the witch. They tangle in fur and puffs of smoke. You see blood fly, and smoke, and you hear grunts of pain and slicing and stabbing. As the cursed creatures entangle in their monstrous battle, you run. Out the door as quick as the wind, you sprint through the forest, the moonlight bouncing from the autumn leaves. You can still hear them. What did you see? You quicken your pace, but as you do, you hear a howl, almost as loud as before, and the grunting and sniffing is mere feet away, behind you. Run. RUN!

WEREWOLF

Common Strengths : Speed, agility, strength, sharp claws and fangs, healing abilities

Common Weaknesses : Nocturnal, silver bullets, decapitation

The poor souls who inherit monstrous curses are usually wracked with guilt over their actions, which are out of their control. The fear of loss of humanity is a sickening reality for these characters, as werewolves succumb to the full moon and must deal with whatever atrocity they commit in the fallout.

On the contrary to these unwilling victims of fate, creatures such as witches are cursed by dark forces which imbue them with otherworldly powers and knowledge of dangerous magic. This often comes at the cost of their humanity, both mentally and physically, as they typically devolve into crones with little empathy and only a will to create chaos. These monsters plumb the depths of depravity and fear, making the lives of others a waking nightmare.

DOG DAY AFTERNOON...

Werewolves

Created by : Neil Marshall
Appearances : *Dog Soldiers* (2002)

Neil Marshall's darkly comic-horror action movie, *Dog Soldiers* (2002), is a clever beast, not unlike the vicious werewolves who populate it. With a ragtag squad of soldiers facing off with the ruthless beasts in a Scottish countryside forest, the film is full of classic one-liners, wonderfully fleshed-out characters and pure, pulse-pounding horror.

The tension of the very real terror they find themselves in is relieved at just the right moments, giving the audiences pause for breath and laughs in equal measure. On the flip-side, the deprecating jabs the soldiers take at each

A werewolf attacks in Dog Soldiers *– @ Pathé*

other make them likeable and, more importantly, believable characters. This provides some genuinely tragic moments, as the soldiers are picked off in gruesome fashion by the giant, lanky and deadly werewolves.

Action and horror movies often live or die by their antagonists, and thankfully the wolves in *Dog Soldiers* are straight from a nightmare. They are fiendish killing machines, scraping with claws and teeth and mincing through the soldiers as if they were butter. There are guts and gore galore as the crimson sprays around the forest, the soldiers desperately trying to make a stand against all of the odds.

Once again, practical special effects are at the forefront, and the swift and tall wolf suits are a marvel, with Neil Marshall's direction keeping them framed just long enough to feel totally believable. He doesn't overuse the physicality of the creatures, but their imposing menace permeates every frame once they've made their appearance. Some disgustingly realistic gore effects give a real urgency and life-or-death feel to the proceedings.

Thanks to a fantastic script and classic characters, the horror and humour take top spots in this completely unique and action-packed assault on the senses.

I WILL GUIDE THY HAND...

The VVitch

Created by : Robert Eggers
Appearances : *The Witch* (2015)

While the Witch herself is only physically seen briefly at the beginning of the 2015 film *The Witch* (stylised as *The VVitch*), her presence and influence are felt almost constantly, such is the foreboding nature of this folk-horror tale.

The story follows a family living in a New England homestead after being excommunicated from their parish over a religious dispute. Their home is on

The Witch (Sarah Stephens) in her human form – © Universal Pictures

the outskirts of a large forest, which they use to hunt, gather firewood and otherwise forage to live their lives. But there is a mysterious force living in the woods, and it begins to slowly influence the course of their lives with a seductive, supernatural power.

Tragedy, questionable practices, the vast, unexplored woods and the stresses of family life all play a part in this anxiety-inducing supernatural horror, one whose setting is as much a monster as the sinister forces that work to coerce the family into dark rituals of appeasement.

The Witch is a grim film, and the main antagonist comes in many forms: a beautiful and seductive forest-dwelling woman, a haggard, humanoid creature that uses animals and children as ingredients for wicked brews, and the disembodied voices of the countryside and the family goat, Black Phillip.

One can't help but feel the dread dripping from every facet of *The Witch*. Its visuals are gritty and grounded in realism, its performances powerful and captivating, its score is atmospheric and its villain is terrifying on a psychological and spiritual level. Far from the cackling, broomstick-bearing

Black Phillip and the children in The Witch *– @ Universal Pictures*

crones of children's stories, the witch is a demonic entity; a brutal and relentless temptress that seeks to tap into the dark desires and fantasies inherent in all humans, especially those who are isolated and vulnerable.

I'M SO SCARED...

The Blair Witch

Created by : Daniel Myrick, Eduardo Sánchez
Appearances : *The Blair Witch Project* (1999), *Book of Shadows: Blair Witch 2* (2000), *Blair Witch* (2016), Various novels, comics and video games

The horror landscape changed in 1999 with the release of the independent found-footage nightmare, *The Blair Witch Project*. Framed as if it were recovered camera footage, it follows a group of three as they interview townsfolk about the legends of the Blair Witch, before taking to the Maryland woods in search of anything to signify her existence.

The unseen is key in this slow-building rollercoaster of fear. The crack of a branch. An odd arrangement of rocks. The strange effigies hanging about the forest like some ill omen...

While some might find the reliance on audience imagination lazy, it's this realism that grounds *The Blair Witch Project*, and the fact that the movie revitalised the found-footage genre gave it an eerie draw in that some marketing led audience members to believe that what they were seeing unfold was real.

Once the legends of the witch are established in the first act of the film, the story rolls with ever-building tension towards seeing those urban myths realised, with spine-tingling, fatal consequences.

The monster of the witch would come into a more tangible form in the traditional, but much-maligned sequel, *Book of Shadows: Blair Witch 2*. It was a more stereotypical effects-laden spook-fest that had very little in common with the atmospheric original.

A third film, simply titled *Blair Witch*, follows on from the 1999 movie as the protagonists search for any remnants of the missing documentary makers. Things go awry again, and in the final act the witch makes a brief appearance. A gangly, ghoulish demon, the Blair Witch finally has her split-second to

The Blair Witch's Symbol – © Artisan Entertainment

Above: *Heather (Heather Donahue) in* The Blair Witch Project – © *Artisan Entertainment*

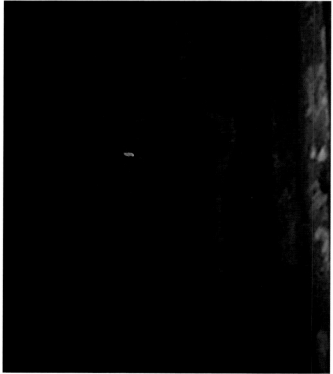

Left: *The Blair Witch in* Blair Witch – © *Lionsgate*

THE ULTIMATE BOOK OF MOVIE MONSTERS

shine, although the film itself is a mess of unsatisfying re-treads of the original film's scares with some out-of-place sci-fi concepts.

Despite the lacklustre sequels, the Blair Witch lives on as a terrifying supernatural monster, and her legend has spread to novels and video games.

I PUT A SPELL ON YOU...

The Sanderson Sisters

Created by : David Kirschner, Mick Garris
Appearances : *Hocus Pocus* (1993), *Hocus Pocus 2* (2022)

Now a Halloween tradition, the exploits of the Sanderson sisters are revered for their meshing of comic and gothic fantasy, providing children and adults alike with spooky entertainment for nearly 30 years.

The three witches were killed during the height of witchcraft in Salem, caught and put on trial for killing a child in an attempt to prolong their youth. Cursing their victim's brother to a life of immortality as a black cat, the witchy trio manage to put an asterisk beside their elimination, a spell that guarantees their return in the future.

In 1993, which is also the year of the film's release, the witches return to continue their hunt for viable children to retain a youthful physicality. With leader Winifred's excellent nose, they scour the town on Halloween in search of prey. There's a fine balance on show in *Hocus Pocus*, with Sarah, Mary and Winifred constantly bickering through their frustration at the lack of fodder for their wicked ways. Sarah is on the hunt for love, Mary doesn't seem to know what is happening at any given time, and Winifred is confounded by the ineptitude of her cohorts.

It all makes for some genuinely funny moments, and the three lead actresses – Bette Midler, Sarah Jessica Parker and Kathy Najimy – give the performances their all. Spells go awry, Billy the zombie is resurrected and

The Sanderson Sisters (Kathy Najimy, Bette Midler and Sarah Jessica Parker) in Hocus Pocus –
© *Buena Vista Pictures*

a talking black cat is out for revenge for wrongdoings from centuries ago. Great sets, witty dialogue and a memorable musical number makes *Hocus Pocus* and the Sanderson sisters loveable and fun. It's perfectly family-friendly with just the right amount of adult-skewed jokes, and despite some of the slapstick mayhem and the hit-and-miss airheaded antics of Sarah and Mary, the visual style and gothic sensibilities manage to make the movie and its 'monsters' atmospheric on a level that compliments the humour.

All of this adds up to a cult classic, one that only seems to grow in popularity with every passing Halloween, as newer generations are exposed to the Sanderson sisters' wicked ways. Their legacy lives on with *Hocus Pocus 2* in 2022, a sequel film that is exclusive to streaming platform Disney+.

THE ULTIMATE BOOK OF MOVIE MONSTERS

LONDON CLAWING...

Werewolf

Created by : John Landis

Appearances : *An American Werewolf in London* (1981), *An American Werewolf in Paris* (1997)

An American Werewolf in London (1981), written and directed by John Landis, is a one-of-a-kind monster movie. Mixing genres in a way that very little films can, it's genuinely hilarious, horrifyingly grotesque and ultimately tragic.

When American tourists David and Jack are attacked while backpacking in Yorkshire, Jack is unfortunately killed, and David passes out in the confusing aftermath. Awakening some time later, David is visited by the walking corpse of Jack who repeatedly warns him of an impending transformation. This supernatural visitation does nothing to prepare David for his dark fate and, sure enough, after more foreshadowing by his deceased friend, David undergoes an unbelievable transformation at the next full moon.

David mid-transformation in An American Werewolf in London *– © Universal Pictures*

David in full werewolf form – © Universal Pictures

THE ULTIMATE BOOK OF MOVIE MONSTERS

One of the most famous scenes in movie history, David's gradual and painful metamorphosis into his werewolf form is as shocking as it is impressive. Rick Baker's make-up effects are absolutely astounding, and it may well be the most well-aged practical effects showcase ever seen on film. It's sure to have you watching with bated breath the first time around, as the stretching of David's skin and the rearranging of his bones and organs places him in absolute shocking agony. Once transformed, he goes on a mindless killing spree, and his victims end up in the same position as Jack: walking corpses that continue to push David towards ending his life and, in turn, his curse.

John Landis created a masterpiece in balance with this movie. Everything comes together from beginning to end, with terrific performances, mind-blowing transformation effects and brilliant, relatable characters dealing with impending tragedy. Rick Baker deserves every piece of credit he's been given for bringing one of cinema's most amazing creatures to life.

BARK AT THE MOON...

The Wolf Man

Created by : Curt Siodmak

Appearances : *The Wolf Man* (1941), *Frankenstein Meets the Wolf Man* (1943), *The House of Frankenstein* (1944), *House of Dracula* (1945), *Abbott and Costello Meet Frankenstein* (1948), *Alvin and the Chipmunks Meet the Wolfman* (2000), *House of the Wolf Man* (2009), *The Wolf Man* (2010)

Larry Talbot (Lon Chaney Jr) is dealing with a mournful time following his brother's death. Adding to his misery, Talbot is injured while trying to save a woman from what he thinks is a wolf attack. His romantic interest, Gwen, tells him that what he battled was, in fact, a werewolf, and that Larry is destined to change into a violent animal.

Lon Chaney Jr. as The Wolf Man – © Universal Pictures

THE ULTIMATE BOOK OF MOVIE MONSTERS

And change he does. The moon brings out the animal in Larry, and the struggle between man and beast is pushed to the forefront of the film, and its 2010 remake. Confronting the previous night's violence is like holding a mirror up to your soul. Larry feels deep regret over the actions he has taken while under the spell of the moon. It's a harrowing debilitation that tears at his psyche while he tries to protect his newfound love. Likewise, Gwen suffers as she struggles to reach out to the human beneath the surface of the beast.

Both versions of the film have fantastic body suits to bring Talbot's wolf form to life. It's not only his retrospective sadness for his victims' deaths that makes Larry human; his transformation leaves him obviously beastly, but eerily close to himself. Another unique Universal monster, the Wolf Man has crossed paths with Dracula, Abbott and Costello and even Alvin and the Chipmunks. If you check out *The Wolf Man*, its remake or any of the original sequels, it'll be a howl!

Benicio del Toro as The Wolf Man – © Universal Pictures

WHERE'D YA GET THOSE PEEPERS?...

The Creeper

Created by : Victor Salva

Appearances : *Jeepers Creepers* (2001), *Jeepers Creepers 2* (2003), *Jeepers Creepers 3* (2017), *Jeepers Creepers: Reborn* (2022)

The Creeper is a mysterious and evil entity who spends his time roaming the countryside searching for unsuspecting prey, His reveal in the original *Jeepers Creepers* (2001) changes the tone of this already tense movie, as the wicked antagonist's true capabilities are revealed.

His popularity ensured three further sequels, each chronicling the demon's horrific hunting spree. For 23 days, every 23rd Spring, the foul creature comes

The Creeper subdues Darry – © United Artists

THE ULTIMATE BOOK OF MOVIE MONSTERS

Anjelica Huston as the Grand High Witch in The Witches *– © Warner Bros. Pictures*

to life and stalks very specific humans, mainly those from whom he can smell the most fear. His reptilian look is usually covered by a large trench-coat and a brimmed hat, keeping his fangs and bat-like head largely concealed. He has immense strength and tucks massive, powerful wings to his back. They allow him to easily traverse the skies and leave his victims with little chance of escape. If he is wounded, he simply consumes the part of a human that he needs to regenerate, giving him a sort of immortality.

It's unknown how long the Creeper has been tormenting the unfortunates of Earth, but his crude weaponry suggests he has been around for centuries. Preferring to play sick games with his victims, he can often be seen in his rusty truck as he tracks them down. In *Jeepers Creepers 3* (2017) this was shown to be equipped with booby-traps as well as defensive weaponry.

The Creeper is an eerie cinematic menace, one that is all the more terrifying for his lack of pattern in his kills. Confidence and lack of fear tend to drive the Creeper away, and mind games are as much a part of his process as the physical onslaught. He has been known to keep trophies and to craft weapons from the bodies of his victims, making him much more than just a brainless monster. Resilient, murderous and calculating, the Creeper is not a creature you want to come across on a cross-country drive... or anywhere else for that matter.

Wolves, witches and other cursed monsters can be utilised in so many ways. From likeable anti-heroes to powerful antagonists, humans afflicted with curses often have to quickly adapt to the changes and try their best to either find a cure or look for something to occupy their remaining days.

Witches, in particular, can be cruel creatures, utilising the living for their own nefarious concoctions. While movies like *Hocus Pocus* showcase a more stereotypical 'hubble bubble' approach to witchcraft, gross-out shapeshifting terrors like those in Roald Dahl's *The Witches* (1990) see cunning and ruthless creatures disguise themselves to prey on children.

In addition, horror masterpieces like *The Blair Witch Project* and *The Witch* keep the terror in the shadows, using unsettling imagery and events to create memorable, atmospheric dread that drips from every frame.

CHAPTER 9

FANTASY FIENDS... AND FRIENDS?

Your sword clatters to the craggy rock as your hand goes numb. The goblin before you is sneering happily, with its crooked teeth and dirty emerald-coloured skin. As he makes to bat you with his crude club, you roll to the side and grasp the hilt of your blade. He tries to bludgeon you, but you sever his arm, leaving him writhing in pain on the ground, cradling the stump that remains.

"Where is it?!" you ask, anger and desperation in your voice. It looks at you with disdain, but nevertheless points with its remaining hand to a massive rock that barely hangs from the side of the cliff.

"Push it", it snarls. "You'll find what you seek. But none of this matters. You'll be dead before you can even pick it up." The goblin spits a gob of black blood to the cold stone and begins to laugh. In a fleeting moment of pure anger, you shove your sword through its wretched heart, and make for the rock. As you push with all your might, the stone gives way, before tumbling and smashing down the mountainside. As you stare at the ruby diamond that can reverse the curse on your homeland, you hear it. A rumble as if the earth were parting... as if the sky were about to fall down on top of you. But no, this is not Mother Nature at work. This is something else entirely. Before you even have a chance to comprehend your next move, a plume of fire, a focused and burning-hot jet, collides with the very rock you stand on. Your leg burns but you just about manage to fall into the small hovel where the diamond rests. Grasping it quickly, you climb out in time to see a hulking red dragon swoop towards you, wings stretched out and a snarl on its furious face. You clutch the diamond tightly, ready your sword, and leap into battle...

HEART OF A DRAGON...

Draco

Created by   : Charles Edward Pogue, Patrick Read Johnson
Appearances : *DragonHeart* (1996)

Draco is the last remaining dragon. Forging an unlikely alliance with Bowen, a knight of the old code, man and beast work together to take down the tyrannical King Einon. Einon had almost died as a boy, but he was saved by the dragon's intervention, and so he and Draco share a fate, through the dragon's selfless act of gifting the boy half of his heart.

This fascinating premise sets the stage for one of the most beloved fantasy movies of the '90s. *DragonHeart* is a classic and heartfelt movie, with Dennis Quaid and Sean Connery making an unusual bond believable through quality acting and excellent voice work. Connery is soothing as Draco, yet simultaneously menacing. Draco is inherently morally good as a character,

Draco (Sean Connery) and Bowen (Dennis Quaid) in DragonHeart *– © Universal Pictures*

THE ULTIMATE BOOK OF MOVIE MONSTERS

but with Connery's muted cadence you get the feeling that Draco could burn anyone around him to a crisp at the drop of a hat.

Likewise, the arc for Quaid's Bowen is fascinating, as he initially believes that Draco's heart has corrupted Einon and so commits to a life of hunting dragons. Watching this stance change is one of many very human aspects of the movie, and while Draco himself was a stunning computer-generated marvel at the time of release, it is the epic emotional drama that is at the heart of the movie.

Draco is a formidable beast, with the usual traits one might associate with dragons. His ridged body and fleshy wings make him an agile and aerodynamic creature, and his fiery breath ensures he is a fantasy force to be reckoned with. Combined with his often calm demeanour and ages of wisdom, it's refreshing to see that Draco is as much a 'human' character in his emotions and actions as the actual humans present.

As classic fantasy goes, Draco will always be a memorable cinematic monster. The *DragonHeart* franchise has since expanded to include a sequel and three prequels.

A DYING RACE, RULED BY A DYING EMPEROR...

The Skeksis

Created by : Jim Henson, Frank Oz, David Odell, Brain Froud
Appearances : *The Dark Crystal* (1982), *The Dark Crystal: Age of Resistance* (2019 – TV series), Various novels and comic books

The '80s brought with it some iconic and imaginative creatures from legendary Muppets creator Jim Henson and his workshop.

In 1982, the first ever all-puppet film was released: a dark fantasy tale called *The Dark Crystal*. In it, the last surviving Gelfling, Jen, undertakes a quest to

Skeksis from The Dark Crystal *– © Universal Pictures*

find a crystal shard which can be used to heal the Dark Crystal and save the world of Thra from the evil Skeksis.

While the film features a vast array of wonderful creatures, the cruel and unfeeling Skeksis are by far the most monstrous. These haggard, bird-like creatures live in the Castle of the Crystal, where they use the power of the Dark Crystal to retain their youth, at the expense of the other citizens of Thra. Their commanding voices and intimidating stature means they are an imposing force on screen, from their fury-filled 'trial by stone' battle that sees two of the creatures vying for the title of new Emperor of the Skeksis, to a disgusting feast scene that is sure to turn a stomach or two.

The Skeksis are the worse halves of the Mystics; gentle sages and creatures that came into being at the same time as their evil counterparts due to the cracking of the crystal. The Skeksis are violent and manipulative and use the giant, beetle-like Garthim to capture small villagers, called Podlings, in order to suck the essence from their bodies to extend their own tyrannical lives.

THE ULTIMATE BOOK OF MOVIE MONSTERS

As is usually the case with Jim Henson productions, the Skeksis are elaborate creatures, and meticulous puppeteering brings them to life, along with some sensational and oftentimes terrifying voice acting. The screeches, cackles and throaty rasps that echo about the magnificently constructed sets of the film really add to the unsettling atmosphere of a ravaged land under seemingly unstoppable oppression.

The Skeksis set the dark tone of the movie and would continue to do so as the dastardly antagonists of the prequel television series, *The Dark Crystal: Age of Resistance*.

YOU REMIND ME OF THE BABE...

Jareth the Goblin King and the creatures of *Labyrinth*

Created by   : Jim Henson, Brian Froud, Terry Jones
Appearances : *Labyrinth* (1986) *Return to Labyrinth* (2006–2010 Manga), *Labyrinth: Coronation* (2018–2019 comic series)

The wonderful world of Jim Henson's *Labyrinth* is awash with monsters, goblins and other whimsical creatures. When the dreamy, fantasy-enamoured Sarah wishes for goblins to come and take her baby brother away, she soon regrets her words and is catapulted into a race against time, facing the mind-bending Labyrinth. The Goblin King, Jareth – played with gusto by the late David Bowie, who also contributed songs to the film's soundtrack, which was scored by Trevor Jones – is rife with magic and deception, and he revels in trickery as he challenges Sarah to reach his castle before time runs out and her brother remains in captivity.

Labyrinth is chock-full of amazing monsters. The goblins themselves, who serve under Jareth, are wonderfully designed and brought to life with Henson Workshop's impeccable puppetry. During the bedroom scene in which Sarah invokes the goblins through specific words, they can be seen watching keenly, before scurrying about the bedroom in flashes of mischief. In the 'Magic

David Bowie as Jareth and Jennifer Connolly as Sarah in Labyrinth – © Tri-Star Pictures

The Goblins in Labyrinth – © Tri-Star Pictures

Dance' musical number, Jareth and his goblins sing and frolic while keeping baby Toby prisoner. The song is not only a showcase for Bowie's musical chops, but for the puppeteers and their excellent work in bringing these creatures to life.

The rest of the movie features some endearing fantasy comrades for Sarah, such as the often grumpy Hoggle, a short and bulbous, curmudgeonly hobgoblin; Ludo, a massive, hulking, furry creature with immense strength and a heart of gold; and Sir Didymus, a fox-like musketeer sort of creature, with confidence and daring to spare. They each lend their aid to Sarah as her quest takes her through perils, riddles and the stomach-turning Bog of Eternal Stench. If you're looking for a family-friendly movie jam-packed with monsters, you could do far worse than the cult classic, *Labyrinth*.

THE SOLACE OF THE SHADOWS...

The Lord of Darkness and Meg Mucklebones

Created by : Ridley Scott and William Hjortsberg
Appearances : *Legend* (1985)

Ridley Scott directed the dark fantasy film *Legend* in 1985. It follows the quest of Jack and Lili as they attempt to reverse an eternal winter at the hands of the Lord of Darkness.

It's a morbid fable, a showcase for many weird and often terrifying creatures. At the forefront of this cast is Tim Curry's Lord of Darkness. While the movie itself came and went without much fanfare at the time of release, it has since garnered cult-classic status, and the brooding and impeccably played Darkness is one of the main reasons. Tim Curry gives one of his many career-best performances as the giant, horned demon, his skin a burning red and his pupils no more than slits. He dominates most of the scenes he

The Lord of Darkness (Tim Curry) in Legend *– © Universal Pictures*

appears in, as Darkness is an intimidating physical presence, moving about his castle with fear-inducing purpose and a booming voice that echoes about his darkened halls.

While he is holding Lili captive, Darkness toys with her, clearly aware of the effect his indomitable presence has on the other beings of the world. His cruel plan to destroy all unicorns in order to bring about unending darkness is entirely unsurprising, as his mortal weakness is sunlight. Darkness by name and most certainly by nature, this hulking abomination is a near-perfect fantasy villain, brimming with power and confidence, but crucially overlooking the determination and heroism of those who oppose him.

The hero, Jack (Tom Cruise), is surrounded and aided by several intriguing creatures throughout his quest: Honeythorn Gump, a woodland elf; Oona, a magical fairy; and two dwarves called Screwball and Brown Tom. These characters help a visually diverse fantasy world come to life, and they each serve different story roles, including comic relief and critical exposition. Their peril-riddled journey sees them come face-to-face with a variety of goblins

Meg Mucklebones (Robert Picardo) in Legend *– © Universal Pictures*

who serve as the minions of the Lord of Darkness. The make-up on show in *Legend* is extremely impressive and, coupled with a variety of practical sets makes for a dynamic world with a lived-in feel.

When the heroes near Darkness' castle, they are confronted by Meg Mucklebones (played by a completely unrecognisable Robert Picardo). This hideous, green witch is a sight to behold, with elongated fingers and a giant, crooked nose. She has all the intentions of eating Jack alive as she emerges from her swamp, but, through clever flattery and wordplay, Jack tries his best to outwit her. Like Darkness, Meg is one of the clearest examples of the sinister tone in Ridley Scott's fantasy film, that, if nothing else, is fondly remembered for being altogether original in its approach compared to some of the more by-the-numbers fantasy movies of the '80s.

GLAIVE ENCOUNTERS...

The Beast and the Creatures of *Krull*

Created by : Stanford Sherman
Appearances : *Krull* (1983)

Krull (1983) is an epic sci-fi fantasy with a vast world, daring heroes and plenty of intimidating creatures.

When the floating Black Fortress touches down on the planet Krull, The Beast within sets about conquering the world with his army of slayers: armoured warriors skilled in battle and trained to carry out the callous will of the hideous creature.

The hero, Colwyn, goes on a quest to find the Glaive, a mystical, star-shaped weapon that can help in the battle against the invading creatures. On his

The Beast in Krull – © Colombia Pictures

journey he comes across many fantastic and terrifying fantasy monsters, such as Rell the Cyclops, a strong and mysterious ally played by *Carry On* veteran Bernard Bresslaw.

A number of helpful characters help point Colwyn and his crew in the direction of the Black Fortress, as it reappears in a new location every

Rell the Cyclops (Bernard Bresslaw) in Krull *– © Colombia Pictures*

The Crystal Spider in Krull *– © Colombia Pictures*

sunrise. Throughout the movie, Colwyn's companions are whittled down in a fairly ruthless manner. Imposters with jet-black eyes and giant, crystal spiders await them on their science fiction fantasy quest across a dynamic world.

Krull is unique for its refusal to commit to any one stereotype of the genres it straddles. While it's very much embedded in fantasy - with seers, a cyclops, changelings, kings and queens and the now obligatory arachnid enemy - it also very much leans into the sci-fi world of the '80s, with spaceships, lasers and futuristic, armoured alien warriors.

The Beast - leader of the slayers and the one responsible for the invasion of Krull - is a gigantic creature, residing in his fortress and commanding his brutal army. He has deep-set eyes, a mouth of spikey, mangled teeth and a semi-open cranium which exposes his repulsive alien brain. When Colwyn finally comes face-to-face with the monstrosity in order to save his love, the Princess Lyssa, he must use the newfound Glaive and the strength of his love to defeat the extra-terrestrial warlord once and for all.

Like *Legend, Krull* is a visual powerhouse of effects, with a decent mix, both digital and practical. While it might feel overstuffed and lengthy to some, it's hard to deny the diversity it displays in the monsters, characters and lore that makes up its quirky, unique fantasy universe.

BENEATH THE PALACE...

Rancor and Sarlacc

Created by : George Lucas and Lawrence Kasdan

Appearances : *Star Wars: Episode VI – Return of the Jedi* (1983), Various comics, novels, video games and TV series

When Jedi Knight Luke Skywalker confronts the gangster Jabba the Hutt in his palace on Tatooine, he is not expecting the villain to relent easily. However, Luke's plans to rescue his comrade Han Solo from Jabba's clutches takes an even deadlier turn than expected, as he is thrown into a pit with a monstrous rancor.

The rancor and its species are hulking abominations, with tiny eyes, flaring nostrils and massive mouths that take up most of their bulbous heads. With long and clawed arms, the rancor tries, and succeeds, in snatching the normally

The rancor – © 20th Century Fox

The Sarlacc Pit – © 20ᵗʰ Century Fox

agile Luke into its brutish grasp. It's a cinematic showdown for the ages, and the design of the beast is one that should be recognisable to most movie fans, even if they're not particularly familiar with *Star Wars*. The rancor have been expanded upon in extended *Star Wars* media, ensuring that their popularity and menace lives on.

The rancor isn't the only monster our heroes must face while on their rescue mission on Luke's home planet. They are also placed before the dreaded Sarlacc, a beaked and tentacled monstrosity that dwells in a pit in the centre of the Tatooine desert. It ruthlessly devours any who come into its proximity, and, as the droid C-3PO informs the protagonists, 'in his belly, you will find a new definition of pain and suffering, as you are slowly digested over a thousand years.'

THE ULTIMATE BOOK OF MOVIE MONSTERS

THE ORIGINAL HARRY POTTER...

Troll

Created by   : John Carl Beuchler, Ed Naha, Joanna Granillo
Appearances : *Troll* (1986)

Troll arrived in 1986 and delivered a comic fantasy with a mischievous creature at the forefront. The Potters (including two Harrys, junior and senior!!) move into a new apartment in San Francisco. Before having much time to settle in, the Potter daughter, Wendy, is beset by a troll called Torok, who uses his magic to assume her form. Harry Jr. soon learns that another resident is a witch, and has a storied history with the terrible creature.

Torok in Troll – © Empire Pictures

With neighbours being transformed into all manner of woodland creatures, like fairies and nymphs, the Potters must act quickly, with the help of the resident witch, to end Torok's wicked plan.

Troll is perhaps most famous for being the precursor to the unrelated *Troll 2* (we'll get to that later), but as its own feature, it's actually an original piece of modern fairytale filmmaking. Torok is a well designed creature, with just enough intrigue and menace to make him captivating, yet not terrifying enough to be a full-on horror monster. There are imaginative ideas throughout, such as the conversion of the apartments into forest-like biomes by the magical antagonist. Reminiscent of other practical and antics-filled monsters movies of the time, such as *Gremlins* and *Ghoulies*, *Troll* manages to weave wonder with mild peril, all framed by a rogueish and powerful monster.

OH MY GOOOODDDDDDDDD!...

Goblins of Nilbog

Created by : Claudio Fragasso
Appearances : *Troll 2* (1990)

The now-infamous *Troll 2* actually began life as *Goblins*, as evidenced by the lack of trolls and plethora of goblins in the actual movie. Fearing the film had no chance to succeed, it was decided to market the product as a sequel to the 1986 fantasy movie, *Troll*, despite having no connections in its characters or storyline.

It sees the Troll 2s... I mean, goblins, in search of humans to transform into plant matter for their sustenance. In the town of Nilbog, mischief is afoot as the townsfolk become victim to the goblins, being broken down into plant-like goo and consumed.

Everything about *Troll 2* is excellent. From the terrible creature designs to the awful editing, musical cues and acting. Like Tommy Wiseau's *The Room*, it should be on the top of anyone's list if they love great, terrible movies. In fact,

Goblins in Troll 2 – © Epic Productions

the child actor from this movie, Michael Stephenson, went on to create a successful documentary called *Best Worst Movie*, and the film has become a cult classic for being ironically, and most likely, unintentionally, hilarious, despite the evil, brown-robed goblins eating anyone they can get their claws on.

TOXIC CRUSADERS...

Toxie, the Toxic Avenger

Created by : Lloyd Kaufman

Appearances : *The Toxic Avenger* (1984), *The Toxic Avenger Part II* (1989), *The Toxic Avenger Part III: The Last Temptation of Toxie* (1989), *Citizen Toxie: The Toxic Avenger IV* (2000), *Toxic Crusaders* (1991 – animated series)

When Melvin Ferd, a nerdy janitor from Tromaville, New Jersey, falls into toxic waste while outrunning obnoxious bullies, he transforms into a hideous

The Toxic Avenger – © *Troma Entertainment*

beast, increasing massively in mass and stricken with unsightly growths on his skin. He becomes the Toxic Avenger, Tromaville's answer to villainy and wrongdoing.

The now classic franchise didn't make much of an impact with the release of 1984's *The Toxic Avenger*, but it's since become a much-loved series, relying on tongue-in-cheek humour, ludicrous gore and cartoon-like characters. Swiftly eliminating criminals in ever-violent ways, Toxie wields a mop, a remnant of his life as Melvin, and makes his home in the local rubbish dump.

The original movie spawned three sequels and one season of a cartoon, called *Toxic Crusaders*, which saw Toxie lead a team of other mutated superheroes against a variety of villains.

THE MIRROR OF YOUR DREAMS...

Gmork

Created by : Michael Ende

Appearances : *The Neverending Story* (1979 – novel), *The Neverending Story* (1984), *The Neverending Story* (1995–1996 animated series)

The tale within a tale, *The Neverending Story* brought Fantasia to the screen and stuck in imaginations around the world with its cast of inventive fantasy creatures and terrifying monsters.

There are arguably none more intimidating than Gmork, the omniscient and vicious wolf that dwells in a dark cave and has a memorable confrontation with the brave hero Atreyu.

Gmork attacks Atreyu in The Neverending Story *– @ Warner Bros. Pictures*

Gmork chills the bones as his bright green eyes shine from the darkness, along with his mouth full of pearly-white fangs. The animatronic is a petrifying beast to behold, and the tension in the scene is palpable. Gmork's knowledge of the outside world and his mocking tone set him up as a formidable foe, and the scene toys with viewers as we wait on tenterhooks for the moment when the beast will revert to his animalistic self, and strike. It's the culmination of the story so far, as the real world and the world of Fantasia begin to cross over in a more meaningful way, affecting the realities of both.

PECK! PECK! PECK!...

Eborsisk

Created by : Ron Howard, George Lucas, Bob Dolman
Appearances : *Willow* (1988)

The heroic Willow comes across a variety of magical and fantastical creatures in his quest to save the baby Elora Danan from the wicked Queen Bavmorda. During the battle of Tir Asleen, Willow tries to defeat a troll using his newfound magic, but ends up creating a monstrous Eborsisk in the process. The Eborsisk is a massive, two-headed creature which rises from the moat surrounding Bavmorda's castle and wreaks havoc on the battle surrounding it.

The animation gives the beast a solid and intimidating presence on screen, and it can be seen to breathe fire and attempt to eat its enemies, giving the already ferocious battle a terrifyingly inhuman edge. The reluctant hero Willow is out of his depth against the towering creature, and it's the Daikini (human) Matmartigan, played with biting sarcasm by Val Kilmer, who manages to stab the beast and end its destruction.

The ugly and deadly beast is only the tip of the iceberg in this classic fantasy adventure, directed by Ron Howard and birthed from the mind of *Star Wars*

The Eborsisk – © Metro-Goldwyn-Mayer

creator George Lucas. Fairies, enchantresses, trolls and love potions litter Willow's adventure as he quests across the land to find the prophesied child a safe new home.

YAY, I CALL THEE FORTH, TRANTOR...

Trantor the Troll

Created by : John R. Cherry, Charlie Gale, Coke Sams
Appearances : *Ernest Scared Stupid* (1991)

Ernest P. Worrell (the late, and incomparable Jim Varney) is a cinematic legend. The dim-witted but well-meaning Missouri resident has gotten himself into all manner of hijinks in the long-running *Ernest* series, from a mission to save Christmas to playing professional basketball, both of which he was completely out of his depth with. In his spookiest adventure, *Ernest*

Ernest P. Worrell (Jim Varney) – © Buena Vista Pictures

Scared Stupid (1991), he inadvertently awakens a vicious troll called Trantor, who seeks to turn the residents of the town into wooden dolls and suck out their lifeforce.

With only a few kids to corroborate Ernest's story, no one believes that any danger is imminent. Thankfully, Ernest doesn't dwell on this, and sets about foiling Trantor's plans to sap the town's population.

Trantor is a disgusting, warty monster, with a tall and chunky body. He's slimy, snotty and disgusting, with two unsightly noses, and watching his antics about the town range from goofy to genuinely hair-raising, with the bedroom scene being a particular highlight, one that might be a tad frightening for younger viewers. Ultimately, despite the general consensus and his perceived ineptitude, Ernest manages to figure out the key to defeating Trantor, and, in a very memorable and endearing final act, it is Ernest's caring nature that's the key to dispelling the malice of this troublesome troll.

Trantor the Troll – © Buena Vista Pictures

THE FOULEST CREATURES...

Dementors

Created by : J.K. Rowling

Appearances : The *Harry Potter* series (1997–2007 novel series), The *Harry Potter* series (2001–2011)

The *Harry Potter* series contains more monsters and creatures than you can shake a wand at, from boggarts to the deadly Basilisk. But absolute despair abounds when the any poor unfortunate comes across a dreaded Dementor.

A dementor on the Hogwarts Express leeches from Harry – © Warner Bros. Pictures

These hooded, levitating beings bring misery and torment to anyone they get close enough to, sucking the joy from their lives and leaving them in a catatonic, miserable state. Harry Potter comes across these imposing monsters a number of times throughout the book and film series, and as the gatekeepers of the

Harry Potter (Daniel Radcliffe) uses his Patronus charm against the dementors – © Warner Bros. Pictures

THE ULTIMATE BOOK OF MOVIE MONSTERS

infamous wizard prison, Azkaban, they are constantly surrounded by plenty of fodder. A particularly frightening scene in the third movie, *Harry Potter and the Prisoner of Azkaban*, sees the annual Hogwarts Express train journey to the school halted, as the Dementors glide aboard to search for the fugitive, Sirius Black.

The carriages appear to freeze, both in time and in temperature, as Harry watches the demonic, lengthy fingers of a Dementor gesture to open the door of his carriage. As the faceless demon edges closer, Harry feels all joy being pulled forcefully from his very soul, and passes out in the ensuing confusion.

The eerie guardians spend much of the year patrolling the grounds of Hogwarts, believing that Sirius Black could try to invade and murder Harry at any moment. As such, there is an unease around the school, owing to the possible invasion of a supposedly murderous escapee, but in no small part due to the floating demons that surround the grounds, ever watchful in their pitch-black cloaks.

The Dementors play a huge role in the climax of the film, in which Harry must conjure a Patronus charm, using his happiest memory to defeat the eternal misery brought forward by these deathly creatures.

SHIIIIRE... BAGGINSSSSS...

Nazgûl

Created by : J.R.R. Tolkien
Appearances : *The Lord of the Rings* Trilogy (novels and movies), Various other Middle-earth legends

The Nazgûl were once men, corrupted by rings of power and now under the command of the Dark Lord, Sauron.

Throughout the *Lord of the Rings* trilogy, they hunt Frodo Baggins, desperate to find the One Ring and return it to their cruel master. They play a huge role in *The Fellowship of the Ring* (2001), always in direct pursuit of the four hobbits who have left Bag End on an incredible quest.

The Ringwraiths in pursuit of Frodo – © New Line Cinema

Their armoured forms are topped with long, ragged hoods, with darkness so thick it obscures whatever remains of their faces. Their throaty rasps are frightening, and they speak only in vague, one-word declarations. In a confrontation on the ancient Weathertop, Frodo Baggins dares to put on the One Ring, hoping that its powers of invisibility will keep him safe from these Ringwraiths. However, it only makes him appear even clearer in their sight, as well as alert the attention of Sauron's burning eye atop the tower of Barad-dûr.

Likewise, while wearing the ring, Frodo sees the riders for what they really are: ghoulish and drained creatures, once men, but now empty, hollow shells. Powerful elven magic eventually gets the riders off the tails of the Fellowship, but some later return, surveying Middle-earth from hideous, dragon-like beasts.

The Witch King of Angmar, leader of the Nine, comes to blows with Éowyn, King Théoden of Rohan's daughter, who partakes in a memorable

THE ULTIMATE BOOK OF MOVIE MONSTERS

The Nine in their true, ghastly form – © New Line Cinema

The Witch-king of Angmar – © New Line Cinema

and epic battle with the demon in the final chapter of the trilogy, *The Return of the King* (2003). The black riders' influence is felt across the whole saga, the gnawing dread creeping up on the unfortunate ring-bearer and his heroic companions.

IT IS NOT HUMAN...

The Pale Man

Created by : Guillermo del Toro
Appearances : *Pan's Labyrinth* (2004)

The Pale Man, from *Pan's Labyrinth* (2004), will live in your subconscious from the moment you set eyes on him. This morbid, horrifying creation stands tall as one of Guillermo Del Toro's perfect fantasy monsters. Played by the always spectacular Doug Jones, the Pale Man remains eerily still at his large banquet table. His sagging skin is white with hues of yellow, and two pin-prick nostrils adorn his otherwise featureless face.

He remains in slumber until Ofelia, a young girl in search of a dagger from his lair, gives in to temptation and eats fruit from the sleeping ghoul's buffet. Awoken by this slight, he places eyeballs into sockets on the palms of his

Ofelia (Ivana Baquero) approaches the Pale Man's table – © Warner Bros. Pictures

The Pale Man inserts his eyes – © Warner Bros. Pictures

hands and quickly tries to hone in on Ofelia. The imagery is truly haunting, as the once-blind creature uses its hands to scan the room for his prey. The screech this demonic child-chewer emits will pierce even the hardiest of souls, and his vicious tendencies are shown when he devours some of the fairies that accompany Ofelia as guides.

The mystique surrounding this monster adds to the dread inherent in his very presence. Adorning the walls of his hall are crude drawings of the Pale Man eating unfortunate children, and a pile of children's shoes in the corner of the room only serves to prove their grisly fates. What remains an uncertainty is how the Pale Man hunts his victims. Ofelia gains entrance through a magical door she creates with chalk, and she must draw another in order to escape the monster's clutches.

So, those being the only gateways seen in the movie, just how does the Pale Man lure his prey? Has every victim come to this bleak place on a similar quest to Ofelia? Or does the stretchy-skinned demon have means with which to infiltrate our world? Isn't that a horrifying thought?

THIS IS HALLOWEEN...

Citizens of Halloween Town

Created by : Tim Burton, Henry Selick

Appearances : *The Nightmare Before Christmas* (1993), *The Nightmare Before Christmas: Oogie's Revenge* (2005 – video game), *The Nightmare Before Christmas: The Pumpkin King* (2005 – video game), *The Kingdom Hearts* series (video game series)

One of the most endearing stop-motion movies of all time is undoubtedly *The Nightmare Before Christmas* (1993). Directed by Henry Selick (*James and the Giant Peach, Coraline*) and born from the mind of gothic maestro Tim Burton, this film is absolutely stacked with monsters from the opening scene to the closing credits.

Sally and Jack Skellington – © Walt Disney Pictures

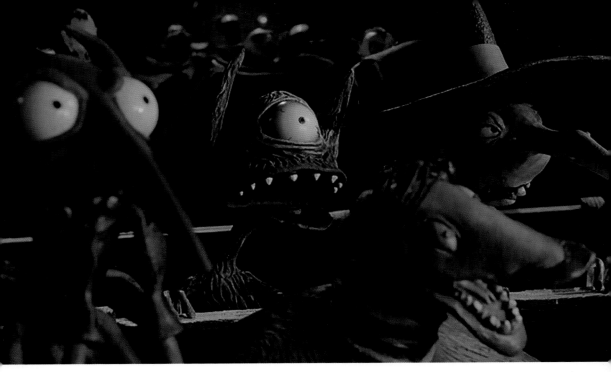

The monsters of Halloween Town – © Walt Disney Pictures

Set in Halloween Town, one of many holiday-themed worlds, it follows the exploits of Jack Skellington, the Pumpkin King, who is the main spook in charge of the annual Halloween festivities in the town. As he grows weary of the repetition of the holiday, he strolls from the confines of the town, with only his operatic singing voice and his ghostly dog, Zero, as company.

He finds the holiday trees, each an entrance to another world and, stumbling upon Christmas Town, he becomes enamoured with their colourful way of life. He vows to bring the joy of Christmas back to his hometown, but what ensues is well-meaning, but ultimately, tragic. Featuring some of the most inventive monster designs in Hollywood, the creatures that inhabit Selick's movie are vibrant, gruesome and hilarious.

From the mood-shifting Mayor, who is literally two-faced, to Dr. Finkelstein and his many creations (including Jack's romantic interest, Sally the patchwork doll), the movie showcases unparalleled animation that still impresses nearly 30 years later. Favourites like the clown with the tear-away face, the oozing Boogeyman and the nefarious, bug-filled Oogie Boogie ensure the film dances between comedic and macabre, as only a Tim Burton production can.

ACCORDING TO PLAN...

The Corpse Bride and the Denizens of the Afterlife

Created by : Tim Burton, Mike Johnson, John August, Caroline Thompson, Pamela Pettler

Appearances : *Corpse Bride* (2005)

Likewise, the 2005 stop-motion picture, *Corpse Bride*, takes antagonist Victor to the land of the dead, where he meets a whole host of undead ghouls and skeletons, not least of which is his new fiancée, the eponymous cadaver he unwittingly releases from the grave with an unintentional proposal. Like *The Nightmare Before Christmas*, the movie is steeped in Burton's signature morbid stylings, keeping a perfect balance of whimsical and threatening. The bride herself is endowed with various frail and failing limbs and degraded, blue skin, and her head is inhabited by a resident worm, who speaks to both her and Victor, of course.

Victor Van Dort (Johnny Depp) and the Corpse Bride (Helena Bonham Carter) – © Warner Bros. Pictures

Victor and skeletons of the afterlife – © Warner Bros. Pictures

The bride's initial appearance in the film is not far removed from an actual horror movie. Alone (or so he thinks) in the moonlit forest outside of town, Victor practises his vows in anticipation of his marriage to Victoria Everglott. Rehearsals have not been going well, so he seeks solace in order to calm his nerves and make a good impression on the well-to-do family. However, when he places the ring on a non-descript twig, he soon finds it is actually the deceased finger of a corpse. As the Corpse Bride rises from the grave and pursues Victor, the score accentuates his absolute dread. It's an effective scene in an otherwise light-hearted and jaunty musical movie.

The jazzy underworld of the afterlife is all neon and toe-tapping musical numbers. Bonejangles, played by none other than legendary composer Danny Elfman himself, puts Victor through his paces with the ridiculously catchy 'Remains of the Day'. The gothic adventure is sure to be a hit with both stop-motion fans and those partial to the wonderful world of Tim Burton.

I'M YOUR 'OTHER' MOTHER, SILLY...

Creatures of the Other World

Created by : Neil Gaiman

Appearances : *Coraline* (2002 – novella), *Coraline* (2009), *Coraline* (2009 – video game)

Henry Selick continued his stop-motion directing streak with a wonderful adaptation of Neil Gaiman's children's horror book, *Coraline*. Selick had previously helmed the massively popular *The Nightmare Before Christmas* as well as a stop-motion and live-action hybrid version of Roald Dahl's *James and the Giant Peach*.

Mostly sticking to the novel's unsettling story, it sees the young girl Coraline Jones move into a new home with her parents. As they busy themselves with work and the move, Coraline finds herself lonely and longing for adventure. After she introduces herself to some of the local, quirky residents, she discovers a miniature door in her new home. Pressing her mother for a key, she eventually gets her wish.

Coraline (Dakota Fanning) and her Other Mother (Teri Hatcher) – © Focus Features

What she finds on the other side one night, turns Coraline's world upside down. It's a seemingly ideal version of her life, but with a few uncertain caveats. Her mother and father are oddly calm, overly attentive and downright eerie. Oh, and they have black buttons for eyes...

The other world, with her Other Mother and Other Father, soon becomes a sinister place, threatening to lure Coraline in with false promises of love and fulfilment. Her new guardians take on terrifying forms, the mother being a controlling and demonic force, and the father being seemingly held against his will and coerced and malformed into a hideous abomination. Coraline realises her parents have been trapped and she sets out on a perilous journey through this dangerous world to free them, along with the souls of children who've fallen victim to the villainous entity masquerading as Coraline's mother.

There are sweet moments to break up the tension, and the soundtrack and animation are absolutely stellar. Laika Studios are stop-motion wizards, with attention to detail to rival the mighty Aardman, the studio responsible for *Wallace & Gromit*, *Chicken Run* and *Shaun the Sheep*, among many others. When talking about movie monsters, the mind-bending denizens of *Coraline's* 'other world' cannot be ignored.

FIGHT FIRE WITH FIRE...

Dragons

Created by : Kevin Peterka, Gregg Chabot, Matt Greenberg
Appearances : *Reign of Fire* (2002), *Reign of Fire* (2002 – video game)

The dragons of *Reign of Fire* (2002) want nothing save the destruction of humanity. When they are unearthed from an underground tunnel, they begin to wreak devastation across the globe, and are hypothesised to have brought on extinction events throughout time.

Dragons in Reign of Fire *– © Buena Vista Pictures*

Various groups of hardened survivalists work together (and often clash) to try and eliminate the dreaded winged beasts. They are classic dragons, with massive wing spans, fiery breath and armoured, scaly bodies, their demeanour a far cry from the honourable Draco from *DragonHeart* or Toothless and his upbeat companions from the *How to Train Your Dragon* series. While the cocky and intimidating Van Zan (Matthew McConaughey) and his crew figure out some of the anatomical weaknesses of the dragons, the heroic Quinn (Christian Bale) is dealing with a personal tragedy that holds back his commitment to the cause slightly, although he wants to see the dragons eradicated. These two personalities clash throughout the movie, adding a realism and human drama to the fantastical apocalyptic settings of this war-torn film. It's bleak, the monsters are ruthless, and the threat of death is constant. This movie is not for those looking for a cheery fantasy adventure.

DRUMS IN THE DEEP...

The Balrog of Morgoth (Durin's Bane)

Created by : J.R.R. Tolkien

Appearances : *The Lord of the Rings Trilogy* (novels and movies), Various Middle-earth legends

When the hobbit, Frodo Baggins, and his eight companions journey from the elf haven of Rivendell on a quest to destroy the ring of power and eliminate the Dark Lord Sauron, they pass through the once glorious Mines of Moria. Now desolate and seemingly abandoned, the tunnels soon force the Fellowship of the Ring to contend with swarms of goblins and a brutish cave troll. The ensuing battle sees all nine members fight for their lives, including the four untrained hobbits, who use their size and wits (and a frying pan) to aid in the fight.

Gandalf the Grey (Ian McKellen) confronts the Balrog in Moria – © New Line Cinema

Once the initial combat subsides, the wizard Gandalf advises that the group evacuate the mines with haste, as they can hear more orcs swarming towards their location. As they quickly become surrounded by hundreds of the creatures, an otherworldly sound and a fiery glow from behind sends the goblins fleeing from the caverns in fear. The fellowship are set upon by a fearsome horror, a Balrog of Morgoth; a massive beast engulfed in flame, wielding a lengthy whip of fire. One of the remaining servants of the first Dark Lord, Morgoth, the Balrog was awakened by the digging of the dwarves in the mines, and killed many of them, slaying the dwarf-king, Durin, and thus dubbed Durin's Bane.

Luckily for the heroes, Gandalf is aware of the terrifying power of the beast, and so, on the Bridge of Khazad-dûm, he makes a solitary stand against it so that his companions might escape. The fight between Gandalf and the Balrog is a classic cinematic moment, filled with fear, sadness and the wizard's incomparable power.

The continuing battle between Gandalf and the Balrog is shown in the series' second installment, *The Two Towers*, and the wizard and the flaming death are seen fighting in freefall before a days-long battle reaches its climax on a snowy mountaintop. One of the most recognisable monsters of the trilogy, the Balrog is a fantasy terror to be reckoned with.

VIEWER BEWARE...

Ghouls of the *Goosebumps* series

Created by : R.L. Stine

Appearances : *Goosebumps* (2015), *Goosebumps 2: Haunted Halloween* (2018), *Goosebumps* (1995–1998, TV series), All *Goosebumps* media, including various novel series and video games

The legendary monsters of the *Goosebumps* series made their movie debut in 2015. Having excited and terrified children in equal measure, the master

Slappy the living dummy (Jack Black) – © Sony Pictures Releasing

storyteller, R.L. Stine, and his plethora of ghastly ghouls are brought to life in a meta-storyline that sees comedian Jack Black take on the role of the acclaimed writer. A neurotic recluse, Stine guards his in-universe books in fear of what might happen should they open. Of course, they do, and all manner of wacky beasts are released, including the Abominable Snowman of Pasadena and the conniving and unnerving ventriloquist's dummy, Slappy.

Taking cues from the original *Jumanji*, *Goosebumps* and its sequel, *Goosebumps 2: Haunted Halloween*, see the creatures from R.L. Stine's books unleashed on an unsuspecting town. Many are deceptively deadly. While the abominable snowman chases the protagonists with a relentless bloodthirst, creatures like the lawn gnomes and sweet-yet-deadly gummy bears pose a more mischievous threat. With the town becoming overrun, pandemonium ensues, all overseen by the calculating Slappy, who wanted nothing more than to be freed from his captive state inside *Night of the Living Dummy*. He is out for himself, revelling in the chaos and taunting the heroes with his threatening wit.

Taking a decidedly comedic approach to the material, as opposed to the more obvious horror of the books and television series, the *Goosebumps* movies play out like a child with a toybox, and it's a glorious mish-mash of frights, laughs and extremely memorable monsters.

MIIIIIKE WAZOWSKI!!...

Monsters of Monsters, Inc.

Created by : Pete Docter

Appearances : *Monsters, Inc.* (2001), *Monsters University* (2013), *Monsters at Work* (2021 – TV series), Various short movies and video games, including the *Kingdom Hearts* series

For the colourful employees of Monsters Incorporated, scares are big business. Mike Wazowski and James 'Sulley' Sullivan are among the top-tier workers for the energy company that converts children's screams into power. With Mike operating the doors that act as portals into the unsuspecting kids' bedrooms, the hulking Sulley creeps in and does his best to terrify the youngsters.

For Sulley, it's second nature. His massive, furry blue body, sharp claws and two prominent horns make him a beastly invader into the human world. But, it's a business. And in reality, Sulley is a cheery, loveable beast, with a gentle and jovial demeanour and a passion for his job. There is never any malice behind his scares: it's simply a job for him. Working with Mike, a tiny, one-eyed, wise-cracking green monster, Sulley is among the most prolific scarers to ever work for the company.

Keeping the proceedings fresh for the duo is their not-so-friendly rivalry with the slithering purple chameleon-like Randall, another top worker who tries his best to outdo Sulley's quality scares. The monsters take caution, as it's their strong belief that children of the human world are toxic to monsters. When a tiny girl, later dubbed 'Boo', comes through the portal door into the monsters'

Sulley (John Goodman) and Mike (Billy Crystal) – © Walt Disney Pictures

world, Mike and Sulley must go on the run in order to protect what they come to know as an innocent and caring little human.

For a movie filled with monsters, just like its prequel, *Monsters University*, there are laughs galore in the misadventures of Mike and Sulley. All of the characters they come across are unique and inspired in their design, and animated as meticulously as only Pixar Animation Studios can. Roz, the sarcastic receptionist of the company is as droll as they come, with her bumpy, frog-like emerald head. Her pointy glasses hide beady, impatient eyes and her long lips are painted with rouge in the dead centre. Celia, Mike's love interest, shares his one-eyed impairment, and, like the legendary Medusa, her hair consists of various snakes. Despite her oddball appearance, Celia is harmless - an airy monster that fawns over the often goofy Mike, to the chagrin of Sulley.

The leader of Monsters, Inc., Henry J. Waternoose III, is a scuttling crab beast who dons a smart suit and is blessed with far too many eyes. Initially warm and caring towards top scarer Sulley and his partner Mike, a shadow is cast over his intentions as the screams begin to lose their power and the company is put in trouble. Once advising and motivating, Waternoose turns more insidious in his desperation as his fears of Monsters, Inc. going under begin to increase.

Revered on release and still loved today, Monsters, Inc. is a brilliant and accessible movie for children, showcasing a colourful and hysterical world filled with ingenious characters. It was followed by a prequel movie, *Monsters University*, and Mike and Sulley's adventures continued in the television series, *Monsters at Work*.

YOU BETTER WATCH OUT...

Krampus

Created by : Michael Dougherty (originally folklore)
Appearances : *Krampus* (2015)

A cursed creature from Austrian folklore, *Krampus* is the polar opposite to the jovial Santa Claus. When a young boy denounces St. Nick and declares his disbelief, he brings a terrible curse upon his immediate family and the group of relatives visiting for the holidays.

With the outside world becoming eerily still and coated in an unnaturally heavy winter, the family soon find themselves under attack from a number of ghoulish creatures – inanimate objects from their household come to life with terrifying ferocity. Jack-in-the-boxes, toothy teddy bears and the eponymous demon himself, Krampus, bring anarchy upon the unfortunate group, and it isn't long before they're desperately trying to escape the hellish nightmare they find themselves in.

Krampus (2015) is riotous fun, from director Michael Dougherty (who previously directed the cult classic Halloween favourite, *Trick 'R' Treat*, and would go on to helm the spectacular *Godzilla: King of the Monsters*), and while nothing overly gory or violent happens in the film, there is still a grotesque sense of twisted dread drizzled on the proceedings. It's a gothic tale set amongst a dysfunctional family who only make the horror more effective, with Adam Scott and David Koechner having some truly brilliant exchanges.

A monstrous Jack-in-the-box from Krampus – © *Universal Pictures*

Krampus is given his due later on in the movie, as the family's grandmother lays out a storybook exposition, with fantastic animation, that details the reasoning behind this horned demon. Resembling a withered old man, Krampus has a hulking and malformed body that is twisted and terrifying, with massive horns that jut from his forehead and bend backwards. The otherworldly punisher is the master behind the mayhem that the unfortunate family must deal with on this not-so-merry Christmas.

Krampus – © *Universal Pictures*

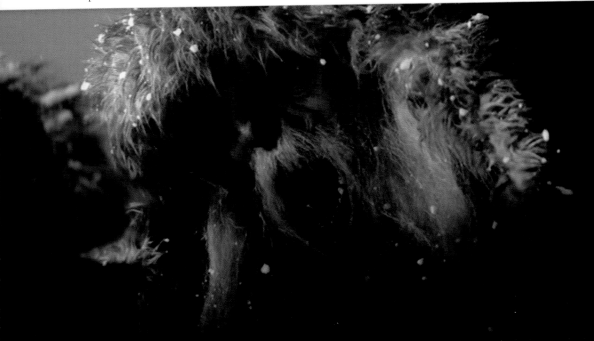

With a likeable cast, a brilliant atmosphere and genuinely creepy creature design, *Krampus* is destined to become a holiday classic, and can be just the respite you need when you're getting fed up of watching *Willy Wonka and the Chocolate Factory* or *The Muppet Christmas Carol* for the 100th time (let's be honest though, no one could get fed up of *The Muppet Christmas Carol*).

AM I KRAKEN TOO MANY JOKES?...

The Kraken and the Titans

Created by : Desmond Davis, Charles H. Schneer, Ray Harryhausen
Appearances : *Clash of the Titans* (1981), *Clash of the Titans* (2010), *Wrath of the Titans* (2012), *Clash of the Titans* (2010 – video game)

The epic tale of Perseus has lived on through countless generations, and was chronicled in the movie *Clash of the Titans* (1981), its 2010 remake, and the 2012 sequel to the remake, *Wrath of the Titans*. The original and the remake follow similar storylines, as they see cities in ancient Greece bent to the will of the Gods, who, after beginning to lose their power over mortals, summon the mighty Kraken, a terrifying sea beast that is so colossal it can eliminate entire cities in a fell swoop.

The mythical creatures in the original, such as the deadly Medusa and gigantic scorpions that attack Perseus and his companions, were animated by the legendary Ray Harryhausen (who was also in charge of effects for the equally stunning 1963 fantasy film *Jason and the Argonauts*). As such, the movie is a fantasy masterpiece with dazzling visuals and a tremendous, rousing score. The 2010 version obviously goes down the computer-generated route, but the Kraken is nevertheless an imposing beast, with multiple eyes, a thick, muscular body and a primal need for destruction.

Perseus fights the Kraken in the 1981 movie – © United Artists

Perseus fights the Kraken in the 2010 movie – © Warner Bros. Pictures

Witnessing the heroism of Perseus and his mighty flying steed, Pegasus, is something to behold. The 'Clash' referred to in the title comes about thanks to Perseus and his companions' quest to defeat Medusa, the horrifying Gorgon. With a thick, serpentine tail in place of legs, a multitude of snakes for hair, and a gaze that can turn living creatures to stone, it is this infamous beast that gives the heroes their chance to stop the Kraken. Their showdown with Medusa is tense and riveting, an atmospheric cinematic battle that is equally engrossing in both versions. It's a classic tale of adventure about a hero overcoming seemingly impossible odds, pitting monster against monster in an epic showdown that sees the monstrous Kraken attempt to destroy entire cities and prevent the heroes from ending the disastrous will of the gods.

WE COULD LET... HER... DO IT...

Shelob

Created by : J.R.R. Tolkien
Appearances : *The Lord of the Rings* Trilogy (novels and movies), *Middle-earth: Shadow of War* (2018 – video game, in human form), Various other legends of Middle-earth

The twisted creature Gollum is supposed to be a guide for the hobbits Frodo and Sam as they make their final approach to Mount Doom in order to destroy the One Ring and save Middle-earth from ruin at the hands of the Dark Lord Sauron.

As he craves the ring that was lost when Frodo's uncle Bilbo visited Gollum's cave in *The Hobbit* series, Gollum concocts a twisted plan to kill the hobbits and steal back his most prized possession. He leads the hobbits through what he calls a 'shortcut', but what is actually the lair of a massive, murderous spider-beast known as Shelob.

THE ULTIMATE BOOK OF MOVIE MONSTERS

Sam Gamgee (Sean Astin) battles Shelob in The Return of the King – © *New Line Cinema*

Frodo and Sam quickly realise that something is amiss, as the dark cavern is strewn with webs and the remains of visitors past. Shelob then hunts them down, her limber, eight-legged body making her an effective and fast-paced hunter.

A frantic escape and battle ensues, with Frodo becoming incapacitated as Sam is left to use an old gift to try and drive the creature back. Fantasy's fascination with arachnid monsters is on full show in *The Return of the King*, as the hobbits battle with the ancient creature, searching for a weakness against seemingly insurmountable odds.

Deadly and overgrown spider-beasts are a staple monster in modern fantasy.

The Crystal Spider of *Krull* is a terrifying creature that ruthlessly hunts anyone who comes into its mountain lair. In *Harry Potter and the Chamber of Secrets* (2002), Harry and Ron come face-to-face with an intelligent and manipulative gigantic spider, called Aragog.

Once a pet of the gentle gamekeeper Hagrid, Aragog now lives in the Forbidden Forest outside the grounds of Hogwarts. Although he does grant the boys some information regarding the chamber of secrets, things turn sinister when they try to leave, and Aragog sets hundreds of smaller spiders on them. They're only small by comparison to their father however, and Harry and Ron barely escape with their lives.

Beyond the realm of fantasy movies, it's worth mentioning other arachnid terrors that have horrified movie-goers throughout the years. A darkly-comic adventure that really shouldn't be watched by anyone with a true fear or phobia of spiders is *Arachnophobia* (1990). Directed by long-time producer Frank Marshall (producer of the *Indiana Jones* and *Back to the Future* series, as well as the future director of *Alive* and *Congo*), the movie stars Jeff Daniels (*Dumb and Dumber, Godless, Steve Jobs*) as physician Ross Jennings, who must deal with deadly cases concerning a Venezuelan spider that has created a nest in a small Californian town. While there are light-hearted moments throughout – John Goodman is on perfect form as the overconfident exterminator Delbert McClintock – the movie is tapped into that inherent fear of spiders so many of us have (Dr. Jennings and his son actually have arachnophobia in the film). If you can handle the occasional skin crawl, check it out, as it's a genuinely fantastic film.

The dreaded creatures are blown to ludicrous size in the David Arquette-led comedy, *Eight Legged Freaks* (2002), where a variety of different spiders are exposed to toxic waste, mutating them and making them colossal terrors.

Aragog in Harry Potter and the Chamber of Secrets *– © Warner Bros. Pictures*

The movie was originally titled *Arach Attack*, and was still released in some European territories with this title. However, it was deemed to sound too close to Iraq, which was a sensitive subject around the time of release due to the conflicts taking place there.

Fantasy allows filmmakers' imaginations to run wild. With limitless worlds and rules they can adjust and manipulate to fix the narrative, a fantasy movie makes for an endless playground. They can blend with classic monsters or forge all new ones, for heroic adventures, twisted fairy tales (like the 2010 epic Norwegian found footage monster movie, Troll Hunter) and mind-bending horror. They can also provide characters with powerful allies, such as dragons, centaurs and fairies. From the clever and powerful dragon Smaug in *The Hobbit* trilogy (2012–2014), to the fun, yet misunderstood denizens of *Little Monsters* (1989), fiend and friend alike have inhabited the wonderful world of fantasy cinema for decades, and they don't show any signs of slowing down.

CHAPTER 10

CINEMATIC CLASSICS

The hiss of the machine indicates it has powered down. You try your best to contain your excitement, but you pick at the handle quickly to avoid burning yourself. The metallic cylinder bursts open in a puff of smoke, the heat forcing you to take a step back. You bang into the coffee table, sending a cup hurtling to the floor. As you glance back you see a shape darting from the capsule. Could it be?

You carefully survey the small laboratory, but there's no evidence of life. As the smoke clears you take another look inside the booth, your breath held tightly as you reach out a hand and wave away the remnants. Nothing...

But as you make to sigh, a growl covers up any sound you had planned to emit. You see a shadow cast over the table in front of you, nine feet tall at least. Knowing your fate, you turn slowly on your heel to see the rat you forced into the booth, standing on its hind legs, its body now massive and malformed, with burning red eyes and 12-inch teeth. Drool drips from its fangs as it raises foot-long claws to the sky. Where once the rat shrieked as you forced it into experiments, now you squeal as it guts you and devours you whole.

Success?

CLEVER GIRL...

Cloned Dinosaurs

Created by : Michael Crichton, Dinosaur DNA from mosquitoes trapped in amber, Jurassic Park scientists

Appearances : *Jurassic Park* (1990 – novel), *The Lost World* (1995 – novel), *Jurassic Park* (1993), *The Lost World: Jurassic Park* (1997), *Jurassic Park III* (2001),

Jurassic World (2015), *Jurassic World: Fallen Kingdom* (2018), *Jurassic World: Dominion* (2022), *Battle at Big Rock* (2019 – short film), *Jurassic World: Camp Cretaceous* (2020 – animated TV series), Countless other media including children's novels, comic books and video games

Steven Spielberg shook Hollywood, quite literally, with his 1993 adaptation of Michael Crichton's innovative science fiction thriller novel, *Jurassic Park*. Following a group of archaeologists and scientists who are chosen by an eccentric millionaire to test out his new theme park before the official opening, the movie, and its subsequent sequels, are rife with deadly dinosaurs having been cloned using a combination of discovered D.N.A. and repurposed genetic code.

The practical effects combined with non-intrusive CGI ensure *Jurassic Park* still looks great, even by today's standards. Like *Jaws* before it, the adventurous series is thrilling in no small part due to the realism associated with these creatures. While conjured monsters can be terrifying due to their otherworldly nature, the terror inherent with unleashing predators from another time is juxtaposed perfectly with the wonder of adventure and the touching interactions with the more docile herbivores of the park.

With chilling and iconic scenes like the Tyrannosaurus Rex's escape and rampage during a power cut, the epic battle between the T-Rex and the

Dr. Alan Grant (Sam Neill) tries to distract the T-Rex from its rampage – © Universal Pictures

Spinosaurus, and the appearance of the mighty underwater beast, the Mosasaurus, the series is jam-packed with fascinating beasts.

While the T-Rex might dominate the discussion and marketing when it comes to dinosaur adventure films, few beasts are as terrifying as the velociraptors. For the first three movies in the franchise, these natural hunters are a constant, looming threat, and they claim a multitude of victims through their stealth and adaptability.

Razor-sharp teeth and six-inch claws, unrivalled speed and clever pincer movements see these dinos cause fear and bloodshed in their wake. The pack hunting, bird-like killers go through their own arc as a species throughout the series, going from the main threat in the original movies, to slightly under control allies in the revitalised *Jurassic World* series. They never truly lose their menace however, and it's clear they will never shed that innate need to hunt and kill.

For nearly 30 years, the *Jurassic* series has brought wonder to families and monster lovers alike. Finding a perfect balance of adventure and fear, this classic franchise has now expanded far beyond Crichton's meticulously researched novel to reach video games, children's TV shows (*Jurassic World: Camp Cretaceous*), toys and theme park rides. The dinosaurs may be extinct, but their popularity sure isn't.

Blue the raptor in Jurassic World *– © Universal Pictures*

THE ULTIMATE BOOK OF MOVIE MONSTERS

BE AFRAID...

The Fly (Brundlefly)

Created by : George Langelaan, Kurt Neumann, James Clavell, David Cronenberg, Chris Walas

Appearances : *The Fly* (1958), *Return of the Fly* (1959), *Curse of the Fly* (1965), *The Fly* (1986), *The Fly II* (1989)

David Cronenberg's masterpiece of science fiction body-horror, *The Fly* (1986), brought with it one of the most disturbing movie monsters of all time. The fantastic and innovative scientist, Seth Brundle, is working on revolutionary teleportation technology. When he decides to become his own guinea pig,

Veronica (Geena Davis) and Seth Brundle (Jeff Goldblum) in The Fly – © 20ᵗʰ Century Fox

he steps into one of the two transport pods, unaware that a fly has joined him at the last second. The teleportation is a huge success, but what comes after is a nightmare of blood, pus and primal urges.

As the movie goes on, Seth begins to slowly transform into a human-fly hybrid, his skin and psyche decaying and his humanity being replaced with the traits, practices and appearance of a common house fly. It might sound innocent on paper, but in reality the movie is filled with unrelenting horror. With Oscar-winning, practical special effects, Cronenberg and his crew brought 'Brundlefly' to life with stark realism – as realistic as a mutating man-insect hybrid can be. Once a brilliant and forward-thinking scientist, Seth Brundle is reduced to an irritable and violent shut-in, obsessing over his work and desperate to convince himself and his love interest (Geena Davis – *Beetlejuice, Thelma & Louise, Cutthroat Island*) that the teleportation has made him into a more pure version of himself.

The degradation of Brundle into 'Brundlefly' garners sympathy and turns stomachs. As he slowly transforms, he begins to exhibit inhuman strength, as

The Fly – © 20th Century Fox

THE ULTIMATE BOOK OF MOVIE MONSTERS

evidenced in a particularly brutal arm-wrestling contest early on in the film. Similarly, he begins to vomit onto his food in order to break it down with enzymes for consumption. This hideous practice is used to even more gruesome effect in the final act of the film, which also features Seth's full transformation into the fly, as practically all semblance of his humanity is, quite literally, stripped away.

The Fly is a morbidly intriguing film, and it features arguably one of the most disturbing movie monsters of all time, made all the more tragic by the very human character behind it.

HIYA GEORGIE...

Pennywise the Dancing Clown

Created by   : Stephen King
Appearances : *It* (1986 – novel), *It* (1990 – minseries), *It* (2017), *It: Chapter Two* (2019),
Various references throughout other works by King, across literature,
film and television

Stephen King's lengthy coming-of-age horror novel, *It*, has been the subject of two high-profile adaptations. The 1990 miniseries has Tim Curry in the eponymous role of the malevolent, child-devouring demon. In the town of Derry, in Maine, It often appears in the form of Pennywise the dancing clown, in an effort to lure children into its vicious grasp. Awakening every 27 years for a year-long feast on the town's children, the creature emerges from its lair in the sewer system to deceive, prowl and kill. The entity is unfeeling and ruthless in its pursuit of its favourite sustenance.

Throughout the series, It appears as a multitude of threats, adapting its form to prey on its victims' greatest fears. The image of Pennywise, with his bright-red hair and mesmerising eyes is ingrained in movie-lovers very souls. Whether it's Tim Curry or Bill Skarsgård, Pennywise exhibits an

Tim Curry as Pennywise in the 1990 miniseries – © Warner Bros. Television

unrelenting malice, feigning niceties in order to trap children, even if he never comes across as overly convincing in his efforts. The tension in any given scene with the clown is thick with dread, as the audience can't help but wonder when the demon will lose patience and strike.

As the split-narrative of the story progresses, the members of the Losers' Club – the protagonists of the series – learn more about the evil being that uses Derry as a feeding ground. In the purest form possible, It is seen as the 'deadlights', shifting balls of energy from the macroverse, a world outside of our own that is home to sentient, god-like beings. It can choose any form it wishes, but more often than not in King's story, the dancing clown takes centre stage as it tries to appeal to the unsuspecting children. It terrorises Derry during the Losers' youth, and again as adults when they return to face their fate.

This monster is not for the faint of heart. With his wicked smile and murderous purposes, It has poised itself high in the collective cinematic psyche, and has given viewers and readers pause when they pass a drain on the side of the road...

Bill Skarsgård as Pennywise in the 2017 film – © Warner Bros. Pictures

EVIL, AWAKENED...

The Mummy

Created by   : Nina Wilcox Putnam, Richard Schayer

Appearances : Original Universal movie series, Hammer movie series, Universal Reboot series, *The Mummy* (2017)

The Mummy... an ancient evil, awakened. An undead force with otherworldly powers and a personal vendetta. He cares not for the needs, worries or opposition of mortals. Imhotep, the high priest, is back for vengeance, and to seek his lost love.

The Egyptian setting of the many incarnations of *The Mummy* is exotic, enchanting and horrifying. The atmosphere inherent in the long-forgotten tombs of Egypt lend themselves perfectly to the kind of slow-burning, dread-filled horror that Universal created in the Boris Karloff-led original. When a team of archaeologists unearth the mummified Imhotep, one of the group unwittingly reads aloud from the Scroll of Thoth, unaware of its properties of resurrection. The cursed creature rises from his sarcophagus, and spends nearly a decade in disguise as an Egyptian civilian, using make-up to hide his decaying flesh.

He searches for his lover from his past life, Anck-su-namun, whom he seeks to kill and reincarnate using the scroll, thereby creating an eternal bride. Like the other Universal monster movies of the time, *The Mummy* exudes a unique brand of fear, and strong characterisations help bolster the timeless story. Karloff is one-of-a-kind in his depiction of the unpredictable and intimidating menace from beyond, just as he is in *Frankenstein*. *The Mummy* spawned a number of retellings in the years and decades that followed, but the most notable, major upgrade for this classic monster was in 1999's *The Mummy*, starring Brendan Fraser and Arnold Vosloo.

While it retained some similarities to the original story, mainly the character of Imhotep and his doomed bride, the special effects allowed for a more visceral and action-packed adventure. Once he has risen, Imhotep, now

Boris Karloff in the 1932 film The Mummy *– © Universal Pictures*

Imhotep in the 1999 movie The Mummy *– © Universal Pictures*

a degraded and rotten walking corpse, seeks to restore his body by draining the life force from others. In some instances this requires him to devour the pieces of flesh he is missing, and the unfortunates who fall into the cursed Egyptian's path end up losing eyes, tongues and sometimes life in service of the walking plague.

As a resurrected blight, Imhotep carries with him otherworldly powers, blocking out the sun and calling plagues of locusts upon the people of Egypt. His cursed visage appears in violent sandstorms that he can conjure at will, and his control over newly-risen undead armies gives him an overwhelming advantage over his enemies.

Throughout *The Mummy* and its 2001 sequel, *The Mummy Returns*, Imhotep is continually opposed by adventurer Rick O'Connell and his family, as they seek to return the vile monster to the underworld from whence he came, also contending with an ancient warrior, the Scorpion King, now resurrected as an abomination and seeking to cause his own ruin on the world.

The Mummy: Tomb of the Dragon Emperor was released in 2008, and this time saw the O'Connells dealing with Emperor Han (Jet Li), a recently revived Chinese warlord whose army was encased in clay and resurrected in 1946. It is a new chapter for the series, moving the action away from Egypt and Egyptian mythology. Imhotep did not appear in the film.

The latest incarnation of the mummy was the 2017 Tom Cruise-led reboot, *The Mummy*. In this modern-day installment, Nick Morton battles against the resurrected Ahmanet, who was mummified alive for trying to

Ahmanet (Sofia Boutella) in the 2017 film The Mummy – © *Universal Pictures*

summon the god, Set. Her quest for vengeance unleashes a multitude of powers not dissimilar to Imhotep. Violent sandstorms, zombie armies and soul-sucking regenerative abilities make Ahmanet a force to be reckoned with, as she rains terror down upon the modern world.

The movie also features a rendition of the classic pairing, Dr. Jekyll and Mr. Hyde, as *The Mummy* was set to be the first chapter in a new Universal Monsters series. The idea was ultimately shelved, but the raw, undead power of the Mummy will surely not stay entombed for long...

IT IS THE RABBIT...

The Rabbit of Caerbannog

Created by : Michael Palin, John Cleese, Graham Chapman, Terry Jones, Terry Gilliam, Eric Idle

Appearances : *Monty Python and the Holy Grail* (1975)

The Rabbit of Caerbannog attacks – © *EMI Films*

In *Monty Python and the Holy Grail* (1975), Arthur and his knights quest for the location of the Holy Grail, but they come across a number of nuisances and they lose many men to ridiculous traps, like the simplistic questions of the Bridge of Death and an airborne Trojan Rabbit.

One of their great challenges comes when the goat-like Tim the Enchanter leads them to the Cave of Caerbannog, wherein a hideous beast apparently resides. As it turns out, the beast is a tiny white rabbit, and thinking Tim to be ridiculous, several of Arthur's knights storm the cave.

They are quickly and brutally slaughtered by the rabbit, who zips about, defying physics with lightning speed and ripping out their throats with razor-sharp, pointy teeth. It's a comical monster scene in an already hilarious comedy. Adding to the ludicrous premise of the killer rabbit, the priests accompanying the knights bring forth the Holy Hand Grenade of Antioch, the only chance to destroy the horrifying creature once and for all.

After a lengthy tutorial, and a count to five... err... three, the hand grenade is lobbed in the direction of the rabbit and, luckily for Arthur and his companions, the beast snuffs it.

BRIGHT LIGHT! BRIGHT LIGHT!...

Mogwai and the Gremlins

Created by : Joe Dante and Chris Columbus

Appearances : *Gremlins* (1984), *Gremlins 2: The New Batch* (1990), *Gremlins: Secrets of the Mogwai* (2022 – animated series), Various other media including novels and video games

We're no strangers to Mogwai. You know the rules, and so do I. The adorable, furry creatures are gentle companions, their soft coat and large ears stealing the hearts of audiences around the world in Joe Dante's *Gremlins* (1984) and its sequel, *Gremlins 2: The New Batch* (1990). But while Gizmo, the protagonist Mogwai of the franchise, might seem cute on the outside, and has a soothing, purring singing voice, taking the furball under your care comes with a few caveats.

With each Mogwai comes a set of rules – not advice, rules. They are to be followed to the letter, and they should already be familiar to anyone with an interest in film: keep them away from bright lights, don't get them wet. And, most importantly of all, never feed them after midnight. While Gizmo's new owner, Zach, is never given an explicit explanation of the possible fallout of a failure to adhere to these rules, he soon finds out the hard way just what the seemingly agreeable, fluffy friend has in store for him.

With the inevitable breaking of the rules, the loveable Gizmo births a multitude of other Mogwai which in turn become nasty, slimy monsters. Retaining the large ears but none of the cuteness, the green gremlins are only ever bad news. Mischievous at first, but soon turning deadly, the gremlins live to breed chaos, just as they seek to breed more of their kind. Whether it's Zach's hometown or the towering Clamp building of *Gremlins 2*, these emerald nasties wreak absolute havoc, torturing the placid Gizmo, who feels adorable shame over the creatures he has spawned.

The monsters are memorable, practical wonders. Textured and creepy, the puppeteering on show makes the characters diverse, and they range from downright terrifying – try not to get a tingle in your spine when

THE ULTIMATE BOOK OF MOVIE MONSTERS

Right: *Gizmo the Mogwai –*
© Warner Bros. Pictures

Below: *A gremlin –*
© Warner Bros. Pictures

you see the spider-gremlin that Gizmo goes full Rambo to defeat – to the sort-of-cute food-crazed Mogwai that devours meals like a wood-chipper. The two films serve different purposes, with the original showing the more sinister side to the gremlins as they dispatch the townsfolk in several grisly ways. The sequel, however, developed as more of a parody, leans far more into the comedic aspects of the monsters, showing an anarchistic rollercoaster of destruction as the pests make their way through the sky-high Clamp building.

From movie parodies, revolting gremlin smoothies and full-blown musical numbers, to chat show philosophers, laboratory experiments and completely unappetising cookery shows, the gremlins are classic movie monsters that tick all the boxes - a perfect mix of accessible horror and memorable comedy.

ALL HELL'S BROKEN LOOSE...

Pumpkinhead

Created by : Ed Justice

Appearances : *Pumpkinhead* (1988), *Pumpkinhead II: Blood Wings* (1994), *Pumpkinhead: Ashes to Ashes* (2006), *Pumpkinhead: Blood Feud* (2007), *Bloodwings: Pumpkinhead's Revenge* (1995 – video game)

Pumpkinhead (1988) is a vengeance demon, conjured up by those who seek a violent retribution for wrongdoings they've experienced. The clawed, alien-like monster has a ridged and bent over, lanky body, with a massive, malformed head closely resembling a pumpkin.

Throughout the series, this monstrous slasher ends countless lives in increasingly violent ways, refusing to end its spree until those involved in the blood debt are eliminated. When Ed Harley (Lance Henriksen) visits a witch looking for revenge on a gang of youths who accidentally killed his son Billy, she helps him raise Pumpkinhead to enact a cruel and murderous revenge.

Pumpkinhead – © United Artists

There's a price to pay however, and Ed soon discovers his fate is entwined with the beast in a tragic way. The movie was special effects wizard Stan Winston's debut as director, and, while not fully appreciated on release, it's gone on to become a cult classic within the horror community. Pumpkinhead's design has been praised, and in the original film, Tom Woodruff Jr, another renowned special effects expert, plays the beast itself. Pumpkinhead is called on again throughout the franchise to murder those that caused wrongdoing to the summoner.

SILENCE IS GOLDEN...

Monstrous Invaders

Created by : John Krasinski
Appearances : *A Quiet Place* (2018), *A Quiet Place Part II* (2021)

The slightest noise – a heavy footstep, a cough, the crack of a twig – and you're dead.

The creatures of John Krasinski's *A Quiet Place* (2018) rely on sound to hunt. Putting our race at a horrifying disadvantage, it's not surprising that the film is set in a near-future that sees swathes of humanity wiped out. The invading creatures, sightless and vicious, eviscerate anything that makes a sound, leaving the few survivors to live in constant fear and paranoia as they literally watch their every step.

With no known reason for the invasion and very few details on their arrival – save for an extremely tense flashback at the beginning of *A Quiet Place Part II* (2021) – viewers are thrust into this desolate world and left to figure out the physiology of the monsters through their experiences with the main characters, led by John Krasinski and his real-life wife, Emily Blunt. Dealing with tragedy has made them even more cautious as they scavenge to survive, taking precautions like sound-proofing and walking

The Abbott family in A Quiet Place *– © Paramount Pictures*

barefoot on sand to try and lessen their always imminent detection. They also communicate through sign language, allowing them to converse with little fear of being attacked.

When the monsters make their appearance on screen, after only brief noises and flashes of grey, they are truly hideous beasts. Their keen sense of hearing is accentuated by their grossly nimble craniums, with a membrane allowing their race to pick up even the slightest of aural vibrations. Throughout the two movies, they are shown to be sensitive to certain frequencies, and Regan Abbott (Millicent Simmonds), the hearing-impaired daughter of the family, discovers that the hearing aid her father recently constructed pains the creatures through its pitch. Likewise, in the second film the invaders are shown to have a weakness to water, which proves to be a pivotal plot point towards the survival of the human race. A petrifying and seemingly inescapable menace, the movies in the *A Quiet Place* series are terrifically bleak, and these monstrous abominations are the reason for it.

A creature from A Quiet Place *– © Paramount Pictures*

DESCENT INTO MADNESS...

Crawlers

Created by : Neil Marshall
Appearances : *The Descent* (2005), *The Descent Part 2* (2009)

One of the most prolific horror directors from the United Kingdom, Neil Marshall continued his trend of original, action-packed terror filled with tremendous creature design in the 2005 classic, *The Descent*.

The movie caught the attention of horror aficionados around the world for many reasons. With a tragic starting point, fantastic lead actresses and some of the most vicious, primal monsters in cinema, it's a true masterpiece of horror filmmaking.

A year after a traumatising event, Sarah and her friends go cave-diving in North Carolina to try and reconnect Sarah to the group through the adventure.

When they end up in an unexplored cave system, things rapidly go from bad to worse. Part of the tunnel they are traversing collapses, leaving them without a chance of rescue. Worse still, something is waiting in the darkness – something altogether evil.

The monsters of *The Descent* series are not unlike Gollum, the twisted and devolved hobbit from J.R.R. Tolkien's Middle-earth stories. The pale-skinned, primal 'crawlers' are bloodthirsty and acute in their hunting prowess. It's deduced during the movie that they rely on sound to find prey (the darkness of the tunnel system presumably left them without a need for sight) and so the girls must move about with careful precision, avoiding both the feral goblins and the fickle structural instability of the intricate cave system.

Crawling about the jagged caverns with ease, these monstrosities are known to bite the throats of their victims with razor-sharp teeth, their rabid energy

The heroines of The Descent (Alex Reid, Nora-Jane Noone and Shauna Macdonald) – © Pathé Distribution

A crawler from The Descent *– © Pathé Distribution*

making it nearly impossible to escape. Evidence of their kills are seen about the chambers of the tunnel system, with animal and human bones strewn around their lair.

Rather than emerging from another world or caused by some sort of man-made calamitous error, the crawlers instead seem to have naturally evolved inside the cold dark of the North Carolina caves, bringing a disturbing realism to the horror unfolding in the story.

The combination of high emotions, betrayal, claustrophobia and the lurking, primordial menace of the crawlers ensures *The Descent* movies are packed with dread, and the films have cemented the horrific monsters as some of the most terrifying in movie history.

THE ULTIMATE BOOK OF MOVIE MONSTERS

A TINY WOODEN PARADISE...

Monsters of The Cabin in the Woods

Created by : Drew Goddard, Joss Whedon
Appearances : *The Cabin in the Woods* (2011)

Drew Goddard took the helm for *The Cabin in the Woods*, an absolutely bizarre and hilarious 2011 meta-horror that wastes no time bucking horror movie trends while simultaneously leaning into their clichés with absolute gusto.

Five teenagers are staying in the eponymous cabin for the weekend, but the events that befall them are all under the control of an underground team, pulling strings and altering the visitors with substances and carefully placed items.

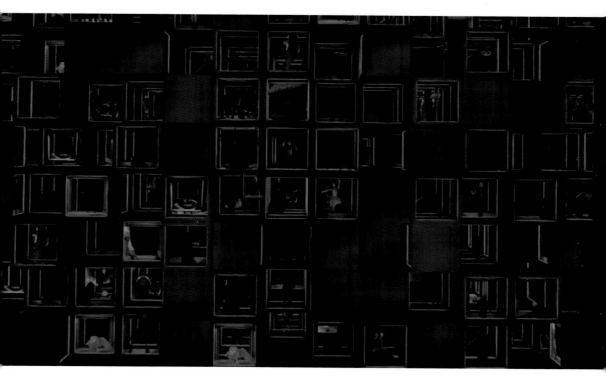

The various trapped monsters in The Cabin in the Woods *– © Lionsgate*

Things go awry for the vacationing young adults when they're attacked by zombie-like creatures. But those aren't the only monsters to take aim at humanity in this picture. The base beneath the cabin is revealed to be a facility in charge of enacting a ritual sacrifice, killing five horror movie trope characters using monsters that are kept in captivity.

As the staff bet on which creatures will be chosen (depending on which planted artefact the teens choose during their stay), a white board can be seen with the possible choices. From deadites, mummies and 'The Bride' to dismemberment goblins, the Sugarplum Fairy and the zombie redneck torture family, the movie is filled to the brim with classic monsters, and most of them get their time to shine by the final act. Amongst classic movie creatures, there's also appearances by some of the more difficult creatures from the *Left 4 Dead* video game series, such as the Boomer, the Witch and the Tank.

The Cabin in the Woods is the horror equivalent of *Ready Player One*, bringing a myriad of monstrous threats into the fold. But as with many of the classic woodland horrors like *The Evil Dead* series or *Tucker & Dale vs. Evil*, it has buckets of humour to balance out the buckets of blood.

PERFECTION...

Graboids

Created by : Ron Underwood, S.S. Wilson, Brent Maddock

Appearances : *Tremors* (1990), *Tremors 2: Aftershocks* (1996), *Tremors 3: Back to Perfection* (2001), *Tremors 4: The Legend Begins* (2004), *Tremors 5: Bloodlines* (2015), *Tremors: A Cold Day in Hell* (2018), *Tremors: Shrieker Island* (2020), *Tremors* (2003 – TV series)

The *Tremors* series is now seven films and a TV series deep, and the burrowing graboids show no signs of slowing down. These massive, tunnelling monstrosities

A graboid attacks – © Universal Pictures

prey on their victims through vibrations in the earth, and any amount of time spent on the open sand will see you devoured without a moment's hesitation.

The original 1990 movie starred prolific actor Kevin Bacon, as he battled the underground worms in the ironically named town of Perfection, Nevada. All seven movies to date have featured the reluctantly heroic Burt Gummer as a graboid expert and hunter, fighting the creatures all across the globe with his gruff and haggard, yet likeable persona, and he utilises heavy firepower and knowledge of graboid movements to best the creatures. Burt has saved innumerable lives throughout the series, but the graboids continue to evolve and take on terrifying new forms.

With co-stars such as Jamie Kennedy and Jon Heder, Michael Gross plays Burt with humour and weight, as no matter how comedic Burt's battles with the gaping maws of the graboids may be, the character had to be respected for wanting to be left alone yet continually coming to the rescue of those who unwittingly, and sometimes willingly (as in 2020's *Tremors: Shrieker Island*, where the wealthy hunt graboids for sport) come under attack from the underground menace.

Spanning three decades, the *Tremors* franchise is unique in its comedy and commitment to its own brand of burrowing, evolving horror.

IT'S ALIIIIIIIIIVE...

Frankenstein's Monster

Created by : Mary Shelley, body parts, electricity, a mad scientist

Appearances : *Frankenstein; or, The Modern Prometheus* (1818 – novel), Countless movies featuring the monster

Amidst the flashing lights and elaborate machinery of Doctor Frankenstein's laboratory, questionable deeds are afoot. After harvesting the most ample body parts from cadavers, the brilliant doctor patches them together and uses electrical impulses and power in an attempt to create and give life to a new being, with all the abilities and emotions of a fully functioning human. Unfortunately, things don't exactly go to plan and, while the creature is given life and the doctor initially celebrates his monumental work, the creation soon becomes overwhelmed and confused by his abrupt new life and the monstrous body he has been given.

Feeling unwanted and aggravated by the reactions of those who lay eyes upon him, the violent aspects of Frankenstein's monster are very much created by the disgust and intolerance of the people he comes across. As much a commentary on societal acceptance as a horror movie, *Frankenstein* nevertheless keeps its foreboding atmosphere through the gothic sets and the unpredictability of the main creature. Boris Karloff is a lumbering physical presence, and the monster in the original film is the classic, square-headed, lug-nut bearing depiction that has become so well-known worldwide.

Practically just as recognisable in her own right is the *Bride of Frankenstein* (1935), a companion creature that appeared in the sequel to the 1931 original *Frankenstein*. Henry Frankenstein continues undeterred in his quests to recreate stable life, but once again the results are tragic, and the original monster's emotions are toyed with even more with the temptation of a mate that is more like him than anyone he has met so far. With her steely gaze and iconic, towering hair, the bride is firmly set in the annals of tragic horror, just like her predecessor. The movie itself, directed by James Whale (who also

Boris Karloff as Frankenstein's monster in the 1931 film Frankenstein – *© Universal Pictures*

helmed the original), has come to be revered as a masterpiece filled with tragedy, moral ambiguity and metaphorical genius.

Mary Shelley's classic and revolutionary novel laid the groundwork for one of the most enduring monsters ever seen, and the misunderstood creature has been the crux of a number of film adaptations, such as the Kenneth Branagh-directed adaptation *Mary Shelley's Frankenstein* in 1994, which starred Robert De Niro as the gentle, yet intimidating creature. In 2015, a version of the story called *Victor Frankenstein* was released, and it explored the relationship between Dr. Frankenstein (James McAvoy) and his assistant Igor (Daniel Radcliffe). In this iteration, Spencer Wilding played the famous creature.

One of the more off-the-wall comedic takes on the creature came in the form of Mel Brooks' *Young Frankenstein* in 1974. Frederick Frankenstein (played by the comedic genius, Gene Wilder) seeks to shake off the legacy of his grandfather Victor (even insisting his name is pronounced 'Fronkensteen') but nevertheless winds up continuing his grandfather's tests on the dead. With

Above left: *Elsa Lanchester as the Bride* – © *Universal Pictures*

Above right: *Frederick 'Fronkensteen' (Gene Wilder) and his creation (Peter Boyle) in* Young Frankenstein – © *20th Century Fox*

the help of Igor (pronounced Eyegor), he creates a re-animated creature, and absolute hilarity ensues.

Frankenstein's monster is immortal in its timeless appeal, and he is one of the most beloved of the Universal monsters, and all of monster cinema in general.

There are now countless movie monsters for fans to enjoy, debate, cower in fear of, and all emotions in between. From pure horror to family comedies to muted dramas, and even massive ensemble mash-ups such as *Van Helsing* (2004) and *The Monster Squad* (1987), these beasts are often meticulously crafted to serve the storytelling.

Arguably, the most effective monsters are ones with a deeper meaning. Monsters that force us to face our mortality as they warp our sense of right and wrong and probe into the depths of what separates humanity from the creatures of our nightmares. In film, we see characters destroyed by monsters, we see entire cities fall at the might of colossal, otherworldy behemoths, and, most tragically, we see humanity itself become the monster; twisted and torn from all semblance of empathy and love.

Yet we are always drawn back to these morbid curiosities, and the monsters of cinema will live on for decades to come.